HOW TO KEEP TIME

A Novel

by

Kevin M. Kearney

How to Keep Time

ISBN-13: 979-8-9861105-1-6

Cover design by Jordan M. Mrazik

Author photo by Sloane Kearney

Printed in the U.S.A.

For more titles and inquiries, please visit:

www.thirtywestph.com

For Sloane

The world, to you and me, is a place of banks and magazines and days that click on schedule. We worry over money and fretfully snatch our entertainment from absurdities. Refusing to take things as we find them, we make up all sorts of fables for our own amusement. Then, when we come upon things that are a little strange or inexplicable, we brand them as untrue.

—Henry Charlton Beck, *Forgotten Towns of Southern New Jersey*

How to Keep Time

Part 1: The Police Station

1.

Every day, Mercer Moore was reminded that it was all ending. It was The End of Television, of Civility, of The Planet. But despite all the warnings, a new day arrived every morning. After a while, he became used to the sounds of the apocalypse. Some of them actually sounded pretty good.

Maybe that's why this particular time didn't seem like the end. Sure, his wife Alejandra had been blunt. She hadn't used the word "divorce," but she had used "I" and "need" and "out," all in a row.

And maybe that's why he found himself in the waiting room of a police station in South Philadelphia, just around the corner from his rowhome. He was the guy sitting in the stiff plastic chair, trying to read a year-old issue of *GQ*.

"Trying" is generous. He was staring at it, occasionally flipping a page, hoping that it'd be enough to convince the other people in the room that he wasn't panicking.

Secretly, he was praying that he didn't run into anyone he knew. He hadn't prayed—really closed his eyes and aimed a wish straight at god—since he was twelve. Yet staring at last summer's fashion tips, he suddenly felt compelled. Not that he was folding his hands or anything, but still: he was hopeful that the words running through his head, words that some might've heard as impotent cries of desperation, counted for something.

He licked the plastic that covered his teeth. It was a nervous habit, one that'd become unconscious in the two years since he'd visited the orthodontist, the one who'd suggested the plastic retainers as an alternative to metallic braces.

"This way you won't look like a 13-year-old," he'd said. "Most people won't even know."

That was just untrue. Even though they were translucent, they were obvious. For one, he had to remove them before every meal, something that was especially humiliating around his co-workers, who couldn't help but stare at the saliva-drenched molds sitting next to his food.

More than anything, though, the problem was his speech. His tongue struggled to adjust to this new machinery in his mouth, causing him to stumble over Ls and Rs. "It's adorable," Alejandra had said when he'd first arrived home from the dentist. "Now say that: a-door-a-bull."

"You wear them for two, maybe three years, and then your teeth are good for the rest of your life," the orthodontist had told him. "Either that or…" he gestured to the x-ray of Mercer's teeth hanging on the wall, "these look a little less like Mercer Moore and a little more like Randy Redneck."

Mercer had laughed, but it was only because he didn't know what else to do. He'd never been insulted by a doctor before, though he wasn't positive orthodontists were technically doctors. The guy had framed diplomas on the wall, but Mercer wasn't certain they'd been as hard-earned as, say, a cardiologist's. He doubted it.

And "Randy Redneck." Was that a play on his name? Was it some dated reference he didn't catch? Was it, technically speaking, even a joke?

"Isn't that an offensive term?" he'd asked Alejandra.

"I've seen a lot of rednecks with shirts and bumper stickers that say, 'Proud Redneck,'" she'd said. "So, maybe they took it back?"

"Still—" He'd drawn the word out, trying his best not to turn his Ls into Rs.

"He said *like* a redneck."

"He said *like* Randy Redneck."

"My point is: it's a comparison to a cartoon, not a classification *as* one."

"And my point is that it just seemed inappropriate." He was not the type to get offended. He was especially not the type to ruminate on whether or not he should be offended. "Maybe I'm overthinking it."

"Good," she'd said, smiling. "White guys should do that from time-to-time."

2.

Mercer had found Alejandra's letter the day before the police station. He'd read the words, though none of them made sense. Even the existence of the letter was confusing: who left behind handwritten notes in 2016?

He ignored the letter's first request and called her phone, which rang four times before he heard her voice asking him to please leave a message.

He hung up and called her sister but got her voicemail. He called her parents and got the same. He called one of her younger cousins, the one she seemed especially close with, though Mercer had never understood why. Half a ring and then voicemail. He didn't wait to hear any of their voices.

Out of ideas, he called his brother.

"Alejandra's gone," he said, his voice beginning to shake.

"All right. Let's slow down. Let's take a deep breath."

Mercer followed Evan's instructions, trying to pause the anxiety that was pulsing through his chest.

"Okay," Evan said. "Now. Tell me what happened."

Mercer was scanning the letter again, studying the handwriting without actually reading the words. "She's gone missing. She's disappeared." As he spoke, it started to make sense. It was the only reasonable explanation. It was the only possible way it could've happened like this. "I think she's in trouble, Ev."

When Evan got to the city, Mercer was pacing around his

living room, explaining the plan: he would go to the police and explain that his wife had gone missing, that he thought she'd been kidnapped, that her captors had left behind this crude letter to try and get him off the scent.

When it sounded like Mercer was running out of steam, Evan asked him if he needed "straight talk." Ever since he'd returned from rehab, Evan's speech had been brimming with new-ageisms: "self-care" was an excuse for his selfishness, "the work" an explanation for any of his personal mistakes. It had all come with the counseling, which, as far as anyone could tell, had helped him. It'd kept him clean, given him the confidence to sustain a mature relationship, and allowed him to rebuild a relationship with their father. These were all good things, Mercer knew. At least that was what he said out loud.

But what he thought, and what he'd sometimes said to Alejandra, or to old friends, or to casual acquaintances from work after he'd had a few at happy hour, was that therapy had turned his brother into an insufferably milquetoast dick.

"I think I'm good," Mercer said.

"You thought about what you're going to say to them?"

"I'm going to tell them what happened."

"What you *think* happened."

There was a beat. Mercer felt the blood rush to his face. "What does that mean?"

Evan opened his mouth to speak, then reconsidered it.

"You've already started," Mercer said. "Go on."

"If you know something, anything, that isn't mentioned in

your report, you could be on the hook. Perjury."

"That's for trials."

"You don't think filing a false report is illegal?"

"If she just up and left, she'd at least tell me where she was going. She wouldn't just disappear. She wouldn't say I wasn't allowed to call her."

"Have you called her?"

"Several times." This was close to a lie, depending on your definition of "several." Before Evan knocked on his door, Mercer had just made his 85th attempt. "No answer."

"Maybe we stop doing that."

"The whole thing makes it sound like she escaped, like I was keeping her against her will or something. I mean, Jesus, Evan. Does that sound like someone who's just unhappy in a marriage? You don't think there's anything weird about that?"

"I hear you," Evan said, his tone a rehearsed calm.

Mercer looked away. He couldn't take the faux sympathy, the self-righteousness bubbling just beneath the surface. If he kept staring at his brother, he knew he'd have trouble stopping himself. It'd been decades since he'd done it. Since they'd had it out in the living room or the backyard. Since he'd drawn blood and caused their father to scream like hell, their mother to well with tears. It'd been years, but he was positive he could still remember how to land a solid blow. He'd never been taught how to punch his brother, so what was there to forget?

"Merce," Evan said. His voice had gone lower, and Mercer knew that this was an intentional move, one that was supposed to suggest deep fraternal compassion. He imagined his brother practicing it in his counseling sessions. Not working, Mercer thought. Not working at all.

3.

Detective Shonda Williams introduced herself and grabbed Mercer's hand for a shake. He sat down in front of her desk, a big wooden boat loaded with stacks of unorganized papers and half-used yellow legal pads. On top of one of the stacks, Mercer saw a framed picture of Shonda and a man with wine glasses raised in the air. They were smiling, happy to be drunk and with one another.

Mercer took a deep breath and felt an ache in his ribcage.

"You wrote down that you're reporting a missing person," she said, staring at the paper on her clipboard. Mercer knew it was the form he'd filled out in the waiting room. "Alejandra Moore?

He nodded. "My wife."

Shonda jotted a note and continued studying Mercer's handwriting. "This says she's been gone for over 24 hours?"

"That's right."

She looked up. "And yet you're just now coming to the police."

"There was a letter, but I don't think she wrote it." Mercer reached into his pocket and unfurled several sheets of paper before handing them to Shonda, who scanned the first few lines.

"So, 12 hours go by, a day goes by…"

"I wasn't sure then," he said. "I didn't want to be overly dramatic."

"Your wife goes missing, but you didn't want to be overly

dramatic." She leaned back in her chair and squinted at the man in front of her, trying to get a better read.

Mercer could feel the pace of his breath increasing, his inhalations growing shallower. "It's what the letter says. If someone...if *you* read it assuming it's from her, then you'd also think she's fine. But the thing is: she wouldn't write a letter like that."

Shonda nodded. Unconvinced, Mercer thought. Absolutely unconvinced.

"It's a matter of interpretation, is what I mean. And after some time, interpreting, I'm confident my wife didn't write that letter."

"You mind?" she asked, pointing to the letter. "It'll only take a few minutes."

"Of course," he said. He studied her eyes as they moved left-to-right, trying to divine her thoughts. A minute passed and Mercer felt the urge to fill the silence. "She wouldn't just leave."

"I know, Mr. Moore," she said without looking up. "I know."

4.

Mercer met Alejandra just a few months after he'd started working in the library. She checked out *Critical Theory Now*, a giant tome he'd used in Senior Seminar two years earlier. He'd spent over $100 on it only to sell it back at the end of the semester for $22. At the time, he'd never even thought to check the library.

He tried to think of a way to mention this while scanning her student ID but didn't know how to do it without sounding like he was flirting. He settled on pointing to the book's cover and saying, "Seminar." She nodded and waited for him to hand the book back to her. Mercer figured this was not the worst possible outcome, but he knew it was close.

After that, he noticed she entered the library every weekday at the same time, like she was working a shift. She sat alone at one of the long group study tables on the first floor with several books splayed out in front of her. While she read, her right hand combed through her short brown hair. She was a sharp contrast to the other undergrads in the library, most of whom appeared to be actively avoiding the texts on the shelves. They wore sweatpants, blared obnoxious music from their headphones, and fell asleep within 20 minutes of arriving. But Alejandra worked with purpose. On her breaks, she wandered through the stacks, her head at an angle, studying the spine of every book she passed.

Mercer once had to trek up to the third floor and noticed

her between N305 and O600, sitting on the thin carpet, reading. His chest tightened—he didn't want her to look up and find him there, staring down at her in the third-floor attic of all places, like the creep who'd never left campus he feared he was becoming. So, he tip-toed away without saying a word, though he didn't stop watching her until he turned to open the door.

It was finals by the time they finally had something close to a conversation. She was working on a paper for Seminar and couldn't find an article. It'd been footnoted to death but wasn't accessible through any of the university's databases. Mercer was at the Help Desk, listening to her explanation, trying to pretend he'd never seen her before.

"I know it's not really your job, but do you know any loopholes? I mean, it's close to 60 bucks for a source I might not even use."

Mercer nodded. "I can try a few things. See what comes up. Do you have a few minutes?"

"Really? Yeah, I can wait," she said. "Hey, thank you."

Mercer smiled politely, as if this was something he did all the time. He walked back to the scanning room, Googled the article, and found the same paywall Alejandra had mentioned. He took out his credit card, clicked "purchase," and printed the .pdf.

He slid the packet across the desk. "This it?"

She clutched the thing with two hands and studied it, amazed. "You made that look easy!"

"Yeah, well, I actually *like* doing this kind of stuff." He didn't know why he said this. He didn't even know what it meant.

"I get that. Researching kind of feels like a quest sometimes." She waited for a response, though Mercer hadn't heard a question. He nodded, over and over again, hoping that refusing to respond would stop him from saying the wrong thing. "Maybe I can buy you a coffee some time?" she finally asked. "To thank you for saving me 60 bucks?"

Mercer tried to remain cool, but he knew that his face turned scarlet when he was embarrassed or flattered. Alejandra had made him both.

5.

Shonda told Mercer that she'd be in touch and reassured him that she was certain everything would work out. "I'm guessing this was all just a misunderstanding," she said, showing him out of her office.

It wasn't until the walk home that he wondered if the detective had actually been sizing him up. Everything she needed to find Alejandra had been written on the clipboard. But if she'd been suspicious of Mercer then she'd want to get a read on him, she'd want to see his face when he spoke about the missing woman, she'd want to study the way his eyelids pulsated when he was pressed for information. Mercer didn't really understand the science of catching liars in the act, but he assumed it was something along those lines.

I should call Shonda, he thought. I should tell her I know it looks bad, but it's not how it seems. He took out his phone and Googled the precinct's number before stopping himself. He'd seen that exact phone call on *Law and Order*. If he remembered correctly, it'd been made by a husband who'd chopped up his wife before storing her in Tupperware.

6.

If he was being honest, Mercer would've admitted that things weren't going well long before Alejandra disappeared. But Mercer wasn't being honest. He'd been taught to abhor lying, but he hadn't been taught to tell the truth.

The problem with their relationship wasn't that they were dysfunctional, it was that they could continue to function without ever realizing how unhappy they'd grown.

They had sex once a month on Sundays between 1:00 and 1:30. The routine had started organically, hungover in a hotel room after her cousin's wedding, but a few months later Mercer realized that they'd fallen into a precise schedule without ever acknowledging it. Like every other weekly ritual Mercer had ever practiced, he couldn't articulate why he felt uncomfortable breaking it.

At some point, they stopped talking about anything that wasn't television. They'd spend hours on the couch bingeing shows about protagonists with highly specific personality flaws. It'd take a week to burn through a series, watching an episode each night with dinner, another one after dinner, and then another in bed before turning off the lights. When they weren't watching, they were theorizing about where the plot was headed, who was going to die, who was going to cheat, and who was going to get something resembling a happy ending. At the end of the week, they'd stare at the rolling credits of the final episode, inevitably disappointed.

But it wasn't always falling apart. There were plenty of good things, too, and this was where Mercer dedicated all of his attention. Maybe Mercer just found it easier to focus on the good things instead of the warning signs. And can you blame him? Warning signs are only obvious in retrospect. If you spend time worrying about them at the moment, people tell you to relax. They will probably use the word "pessimistic." Or, if they're interested in really poking you, they might use the word "paranoid." No one called Mercer those things. And it's all because he focused on the good things.

Like how they spent summer nights on the stoop, drinking tall boys of cheap beer so cold they tasted like ice water and trading neighborhood gossip with Charlene, the woman on the other side of the street who looked both ways before dishing. "You didn't hear it from me…" she'd start.

Or those winter Saturdays when Alejandra would lay eggs on tortillas from 9th Street or Mercer would fumble his way through a Googled recipe for biscuits and gravy, overly confident thanks to an unnaturally strong pot of coffee. Afterward, Mercer would read the maximum amount of free *Inquirer* articles on his phone while Alejandra caught up with her younger cousins' emails. It wasn't tremendously exciting, but that wasn't the point. They were with one another. *That* was the point.

Back when things were really, truly, objectively good, they would joke about breaking up. At the time, it seemed impossible, which is why they found it so funny.

“When I leave you, I’m finally going to be able to watch *Real Housewives* without being judged,” Alejandra would say.

“When I leave you, my new wife will pay for everything. She’ll probably make me quit my job,” Mercer would say.

“That’s adorable,” Alejandra would respond with a smile. “You think someone else would put up with you?”

7.

When Alejandra first asked about his parents, Mercer led with the fact that they went to church every week. Alejandra remembered her freshman year roommate, a sweet evangelical girl who was legitimately terrified any time Alejandra returned to the room drunk. "So, they're true believers," Alejandra said.

Mercer thought for a second. "I don't know. There's a chance."

"How would you not know?"

Mercer shrugged. "I don't know that we've ever really talked about it."

"They raised you Catholic. And they go to Mass every Sunday…"

"Usually Saturdays. Shorter services. Smaller crowd."

Mercer and his brother had spent most of their lives in Catholic schools. He told her that he could still recite almost every Catholic prayer by memory, and some in Latin. The fact that he didn't know whether or not his parents believed in God seemed impossible.

"They're Irish-Catholic," he told her, as if that was all that needed to be said.

"My mom's Mexican and my dad's Italian. They were both raised Catholic. I don't see your point."

"Being Irish-Catholic doesn't mean you believe in God."

She laughed but stopped when she realized he wasn't kidding. "Then walk me through this. What's it mean to be

Irish-Catholic?" She grabbed a pen and a scrap of paper. "Feel like I need to take notes so I can practice meeting your parents."

"So, we're like that, now? You're going to meet my parents?"

Alejandra smiled. "I'd like to think so."

"Alright. Well. You say the prayers, obviously. You fear the nuns." He paused, grinning as he stroked his chin like a Classics professor. "And, perhaps most importantly, you learn to be quiet."

8.

"You're going to think it's loud," Alejandra warned Mercer before his first dinner at her parents' place. "Italian-Mexican-Catholics. Different beast from Irish-Catholics. Louder register. Better food."

"*Wannabe* Catholics."

Alejandra smiled. "Who would want to be Catholic?"

Her mother greeted him at the door with kisses on the cheek. Her father offered him a handshake that felt like a death grip. "The Irishman!" he screamed, and the whole family laughed. Mercer figured he should, too.

The meal was as loud as Alejandra had warned him it would be, but it was also warm. They asked about Mercer's job and Alejandra's progress on her thesis. Her parents talked about how they first met, holding each other's hands as they recalled the details from decades before. The smell of Mrs. Bianchi's homemade meal permeated everything.

It wasn't until he'd begun spending time with Alejandra that Mercer was able to see his family through someone else's eyes. Before Alejandra, he hadn't realized that his dad and mom couldn't stomach silence unless they specifically requested it. The most jarring epiphany was that every Moore was fluent in a carefully constructed language of euphemism. By the time they were engaged, it was impossible to ignore. Out loud, Evan wasn't in rehab; he was 'away.' Brigid didn't disapprove of Alejandra's wedding dress, it was just 'interesting.'

It was a cardinal sin to raise grievances while the family was together—why spoil the moment? Couldn't it wait? Couldn't we talk about this later?

9.

There were only a few blocks left on his walk home from the police station when Mercer remembered he hadn't eaten. He turned left, heading towards Triangle Tavern. Inside, he ordered a Lager and a roast pork sandwich, the same thing he'd ordered two weeks earlier when he and Alejandra had celebrated the start of another weekend. He wondered if there was some sort of clue about her disappearance in that memory, but all he could remember was how she'd laughed at the way her mild wings had made him sweat.

"Do they give you a headache?" It was the bartender. She was pointing to her own teeth, but Mercer knew she was asking about his plastic ones.

"I've gotten used to it," he said, removing them from his mouth and placing them down on a napkin. The accumulated spit looked like a bubbly moat. "Do you want to try them out?"

The woman couldn't hide her horror. Mercer apologized three times in a row, even though he knew it was useless trying to explain that he'd meant it as a joke. She said it was fine but then turned to the T.V., pretending to watch the daytime news on mute.

In between sips of his Lager, Mercer took out that day's index card and crossed off what he'd completed.

A	M
TO DO (6/29/2016)	COLLECTED
~~• Police station open at 9~~	DET. Williams
~~→ Det. Shonda Williams (Missing Persons)~~	215-419-2489
• Call Evan back	Call if any developments, otherwise she'll call in next few days

Usually, when he drew lines through the day's objectives he felt a ping of satisfaction, but on that day all he felt was the beer tearing away at the enamel of his naked teeth. The crisp, black lines he drew didn't mean that anything had been resolved. They were just splotches of ink.

10.

When he was 14, Mercer's father taught him the importance of time. They were in his dad's office, a dimly lit room that held a desk, a dozen cardboard boxes, and little else. For the previous tenants, the room was a walk-in closet. For the Moore boys, it was where you wound up when you were in deep shit.

Mercer's report card, according to his father, was "lackluster at best." Mercer nodded—he knew it was true. Two Bs and five variations of the letter C. He'd been dreading the moment since grades closed a week earlier.

"You're smart. I know that. But you're disorganized," his father said, and Mercer nodded again, though he didn't know that he agreed. High school was overwhelming—too many classes, too many teachers, too many Latin declensions—but it wasn't a question of organization. He knew where everything was. He knew what he needed to do; he just couldn't keep up. Evan had made it look easy. Honors classes and a 4.0 without ever appearing to do homework. It seemed impossible. It *was* impossible. And yet that was Evan.

Mercer's dad handed him a navy book about the size of an index card and told him to flip through it. He worried it was a book of checks—that his dad was demanding he use what remained of his Confirmation money to cover tuition if he was going to settle for such piss-poor grades. "St. Luke's isn't a charity," his mom reminded him once a month when she made the payments. But there were no checks, just days of the week and numbers running down the left-hand margin.

"Here's mine," his father said and removed another book from his pocket. One with a scratched cover and dog-eared pages. He opened to a random page and pointed to the crossed-out, cryptic notes about meetings and phone calls and appointments and lunches in black and blue and green ink. Every inch of every day was monopolized, the many different inks weighing down the cheap paper. Mercer looked back at his own clean book and studied the page.

6 AM	1 PM
7 AM	2 PM
8 AM	3 PM
9 AM	4 PM
10 AM	5 PM
11 AM	6 PM
12 PM	7 PM

Every waking hour had earned its own place. Every one was just as important as the next. Mercer had never realized a period of time could have so much potential. He followed his dad's advice and wrote down the deadlines for the next morning.

6 AM	1 PM
7 AM	2 PM
8 AM	3 PM
9 AM History Quiz (H.R.E.)	4 PM
10 AM Latin h.w. collected	5 PM
11 AM	6 PM
12 PM	7 PM

It was so small on the page, small enough to fit in the squares and inside the breast pocket of his St. Luke's sport coat. "Most people don't realize that it's all about keeping track of your time," his dad said, putting his own book back in his pocket. "It's about being efficient. Be careful. I mean really careful, Merce. Precise. Otherwise, it'll slip right by."

Mercer took his dad's advice, diligently breaking his days into hour intervals and working backward to determine how he'd meet each goal. He was surprised how much he enjoyed it. He still hated the schoolwork, but he relished the jolt that came with drawing the straight lines. As the days went on, Mercer began filling the margins with eavesdropped conversations and inside jokes. In November, there was a list of albums to download on Kazaa; in December, there was the number of a girl from Camden Catholic. All of it was beyond the planner's grid, floating in the blank space between the formatting and the end of the page, outside of time.

11.

Over the years, Mercer worked his way up the library hierarchy. Technically, he wasn't a librarian, though he didn't mention that when people asked about his job. The truth was more complicated and, somehow, more boring. By the time Alejandra left him the letter, his official title was Custodian for University Archives and Digitization, which was a generous way of saying that he spent his weekdays scanning old, unread books before they were sent to the trash.

He had not gone to library school like many of his co-workers, though he'd always loved books. He'd read and re-read Tolkien obsessively when he was younger and would bring the books everywhere, sneaking in a chapter during math class or a few pages in the car on the way to soccer. After he'd read *The Return of the King* for the third time, he began selecting books at random from his parents' library shelves. He didn't care what he was reading—one day it was Herman Hesse, the next Benjamin Spock. The words were irrelevant. It was the physicality that he loved: the sensation of running his thumb along hundreds of pages in just a few seconds, the way the paper smelled like his grandmother's attic in June, the feeling of the spine gradually bending like wood under water.

He knew that his position had not been created to "bring the humanities into the 21st century," as the job listing had claimed. "Digital archiving" was a nice phrase, but it was just a cover for the university's actual plans to empty the library of its books and rebrand the space as a "Communication Hub." It was the kind of plan that would've enraged him when he first started working there, back when he felt comfortable earning enough for rent and a few cases of shitty beer. But by the time he became Custodian, he believed any stable job would require him to swallow some principles. The best of them at least provided a fancy title.

Whenever they fought, Mercer told Alejandra she was upset because she hated her job. "You're projecting," she'd say, and Mercer would throw his arms up, like there was no way to reason with her.

She wasn't wrong. He spent at least an hour of every workday scrolling through employment postings, trying to imagine himself in different jobs, different careers, different cities. He created a LinkedIn profile after reading a blog post entitled "How To Get Hired TODAY," but all he found were offers to teach English in China and a few Russian women telling him he could earn "EASY $." Everyone was posting disjointed fragments and blurry memes about hard work. It reminded Mercer of the old internet: of dorky sincerity, virus-ridden chain emails, and CD-ROMs promising 50 free hours of America Online.

Dane was the only real person to message Mercer on LinkedIn. He'd also graduated from St. Luke's, but the lone detail about him Mercer could recall was that he'd shown up to one of the mixers hammered off banana liqueur and had to have his stomach pumped by some EMTs while the Dean of Students and Principal nervously looked on. After that, he was known around school as Banana Boy. So, no, Mercer explained to Alejandra, he wasn't going to take him up on the invitation to get coffee and talk about a "potential business opportunity."

"He was a teenager. Everyone is dumb at that age," Alejandra had said.

"But he's Banana Boy."

"And he wants to give you a job."

"A job working for Banana Boy."

"A job that isn't at the library."

Mercer knew she had a point, though what Dane actually did was unclear. According to LinkedIn, he was employed by Transformational Talks LLC. He also happened to be the company's CEO, CFO, and Head of Interface. Their website featured a photo of Dane, in a black t-shirt and black jeans, speaking to an auditorium full of middle schoolers. Below the image, it asked, "Are you ready to change some lives?" Mercer knew he was not.

The only reason he'd agreed to go was because turning it down would've confirmed Alejandra's theory that he was content with being miserable at the library. She was right, of course, but he didn't want her to know that.

Mercer met him at an overpriced coffee shop in Center City. When Dane asked what he was looking for in a career, Mercer didn't know what to say. He was surprised to find that he'd never thought to ask himself the same question. "Better pay, I guess. Something that feels like I'm making a difference."

Dane smiled. "When I saw your name on the St. Luke's alumni page, I just had this feeling. It's why I reached out. I don't often do cold messages like that, but I just had this sense that this was a good fit." He launched into his pitch, one that Mercer could tell had been recited hundreds of times. Banana Boy framed it as a revolutionary resource for schools looking to combat the social ills of the present—mental illness, school shootings, addiction, racism, homophobia—though, as far as Mercer could tell, it was really just a company that offered programming for school assemblies. "And, when I saw your page, I just thought: 'the Mercer I remember is a special guy. He has a unique perspective. He has an interesting way of seeing the world.'"

Mercer couldn't recall any conversation he'd had with Dane, let alone one that would've been so intimate, but he was happy to have his ego puffed. He nodded along.

"Your brother, Evan, was the year ahead of me, right?"

Mercer was quiet for a beat. "He was."

"And I heard that he ran into some problems in college, right? I don't mean to be rude. And please correct me if I'm wrong."

"He's working on it."

"You probably remember my problems back in school. Rehab for a little while, then out-patient for a long while. I was fucked *up* back then, man. Still had to take Latin, though. Can you believe that?"

Mercer laughed along with him, though he was disappointed: all of the grim context was ruining the nickname for him.

"Listen. I'm not trying to be inappropriate by bringing up your brother. I'm not gossiping. We roll in similar circles if you know what I mean."

Mercer nodded knowingly, as if this was something he and his brother talked about often.

"But I reached out to you, not your brother. I think a lot of our clients are dealing with addiction indirectly—through their parents, friends, siblings, whoever. They're experiencing real pain, but they don't know how to process it. In fact, they might even feel guilty about that pain." He paused. "Is anything I'm saying resonating?"

Mercer imagined telling a room full of tweens about the time his brother threw up in his sleep. He pictured himself trying to explain what it feels like to accept that your brother wouldn't make it past 40. The whole enterprise felt improper, maybe even treasonous, like he was trading in family shame for a 401(k) and some heavy matte business cards.

"I've never been much of a speaker," he told Dane.

12.

Alejandra didn't understand why he wouldn't just work for his father.

"It's a tech company."

"It's a tech *help* company."

"I have a degree in literature."

"And your brother has four and a half semesters of a degree in philosophy. Didn't stop him."

She was right, he knew that. There was always a job waiting for him. His father hadn't said so outright, but his suggestions couldn't have been clearer. Whenever there was talk of budget cuts at the university or tedious responsibilities added to Mercer's job description, his dad would shake his head. "You let me know if there's anything I can do," he'd say. "Always a way out."

Working at Moore Tech would've been a fine gig—all the PTO he could want, an actual salary, and relatively low-stakes day-to-day. Any time he heard his dad or brother talk about a client, it always seemed to be a grandfather who wanted to sign up for Facebook or a widow who'd been told she needed an email address. He was willing to bet no matter how incompetent they were, Moore Tech's elderly clientele was probably easier to deal with than the privileged pricks at the university.

But Mercer cringed at the thought of telling people he worked for the company his father had built. He knew they'd make assumptions about how he'd been handed things his whole life, how he'd had the luxury of fucking off for a few years before finally chomping down on his silver spoon.

"You make it sound like a global corporation," Alejandra told him. "It's a two-room office in National Park, New Jersey."

Mercer laughed, said she was right, and changed the subject. There was something else, though Mercer didn't know how to explain it to Alejandra. Evan needed the job. It was good for him to have something steady out of rehab and Mercer supposed it was good that he reported to their father every morning, too.

Mercer didn't need that. The library wasn't a dream job, but neither was installing Norton Anti-Virus on the desktops of the nearly dead.

When their dad set a retirement date, Evan asked Mercer if he wanted a job. "Come work for me," he said. Mercer knew his brother was trying to be helpful, that in an indirect way he was trying to repair some of what had been destroyed over the last few years. But there was something inside of him, something he knew was immature and petty and illogical, telling him to turn it down.

It whispered to him as his brother offered him the job. It sounded so sweet. It said, "Fuck you, Evan."

13.

He'd stopped keeping a planner by the time he started working at the library. College lacked the structure of St. Luke's and an hour-by-hour breakdown of every day of the week suddenly felt unnecessarily strict. That was when he replaced his dad's planners with unruled index cards. The morning's tasks were on the front and the evening's on the back, with half of each side devoted to what Mercer had always felt was the most important part of his ritual: the collected the odds and ends of each day.

When he got home from the police station, he took another look at that day's card and updated it accordingly.

A	M
TO DO (6/29/2016)	COLLECTED
~~· Police station opens at 9~~ ~~→ Det. Shonda Williams (Missing Persons)~~ · Call Evan back	DET. Williams 215-419-2489 Call if any developments, otherwise she'll call in next few days

P | M

TO DO	COLLECTED
· ~~Call Maria again~~	"When the aforementioned grizzly issues rapt/ from the bushes, what you do may influence what// he does: I don't know what you should do: I/ think I heard you should be still and not// scream"
· ~~Call Bianchis again~~	—AR Ammons
· ~~Call the cousins Los Tios, Andrea, etc~~	
· ~~Call her work~~	
· Call	

Every morning he'd file the previous day's card in a shoebox on the top of his dresser, like his own personal catalog. He rarely consulted them after the day had passed, but he was comforted by the fact that he could.

This was the card from two weeks before he married Alejandra:

A | M

TO DO (5/10/2014)	COLLECTED
· Abs before work	· Saw guy from tennis team steal stapler
· ~~Bring refill K cups~~	· Receipt on ground for 18 individual tubes of chapstick
· ~~10:15 mtg w/ IT~~	
· ~~Restock 3F stacks~~	
· ~~Front desk 11-12~~	

P | M

TO DO
- ~~Acme run~~
  - ~~Almond milk (no vanilla)~~
  - ~~bag o salad~~
  - ~~bread~~
  - ~~PB~~
  - ~~toothpaste~~
- ~~Prep tomorrow's Complexes~~
- No phone after 7
- ~~Credit union re: car~~

COLLECTED

Why don't I know how to grill?

"You never call your brother anymore"
- Mom

"You never call me anymore"
- Also Mom

This was the day Alejandra interviewed for a promotion:

A | M

TO DO (10/30/2015)
- 75 push ups before work
- ~~Wish Alejandra good luck~~
- ~~Bag of candy~~
- ~~Apply to 2 jobs~~
  (1 - will do other later)

COLLECTED

"...I don't see someone interested in serving God, I see someone interested in being God"
- F Bruni in NYT

- Big Country - "In a Big Country" on drive in
  - dumb, ridiculous, great

P	M
TO DO	COLLECTED
· ~~Follow up w/History Dept.~~ · ~~Return Dad's call~~ · ~~Read~~ · ~~Block Twitter~~	"My sister is the most miserable happy person I know" —Alejandra "This/is not a poem about a dream,/though it could be" —Mary Oliver

And this was the day before she disappeared:

A	M
TO DO (6/26/2016)	COLLECTED
- Up before 8 · ~~Read entire News section~~ · No phone before noon · Run/~~workout~~ · ~~Help w/ Block Cleanup~~	Drunk Ant called me a "do-gooder" from his stoop—surprise! He was drunk No one took credit for 4 used condoms near sewage drain

P	M
TO DO	COLLECTED
· ~~Watch Phils w/ Dad~~ + Evan	"Your brother said something came up. It's the girl, Colleen. Sorry, the woman." - Dad, of course
· Read	"Fate is a bad writer Lucky numbers: 17, 8, 61" - Fortune from China Garden
· ~~Drink 64oz of water~~	
· less than 2hrs on phone	

That night, he re-read and re-re-read and re-re-re-read the card. He had done everything he needed to do, he thought. He had done almost everything that he needed to do. He should take some comfort in that, he thought, but he instead kept looking for something else to do.

14.

Of course, they fought. Every couple did. There was his mom's speech at their wedding, the one about Mercer's 'purity.' "It was weird," Alejandra said months later. "Can we just admit that it was weird?"

There was Christmas Eve 2014, the one where Evan showed up drunk to midnight Mass. "You know what my family does on Christmas Eve?" Alejandra asked after they cleaned up Evan's vomit from the backseat of her car. "We open gifts."

There was her high school reunion, the uncomfortable dinner party at her mentor's house, and the way Mercer always seemed to prefer dicking around on his phone to talking with her family.

"Space is important," Mercer had told a friend who was planning on moving in with his partner. "Disagreements usually blow over by just hitting pause and finding some space."

He hoped the same was true now that she'd gone missing—that the next morning he'd wake to find her in the kitchen, drinking coffee and scrolling through headlines, smiling when she noticed him.

"Can we just forget all of this?" he imagined her saying. And he knew he would.

15.

He figured the best thing he could do was carry on like normal, like his world wasn't slipping away from him, so he went to work that next morning after the police station. He shouldn't have, of course, especially because he was scheduled to visit an Intro to Composition class to demonstrate the many research tools the library offered. It was a summer course the week before the 4th. No one would've blinked if he'd canceled. In fact, students would've been grateful.

He should've lied to the adjunct and said he was sick. He should've told her to recite the incredibly long-winded research guide on the library website. "Consider having them annotate it," he could've said. "Consider it an opportunity to enhance your pedagogy." He should've spent the morning in the library's backroom, cordoned off from social interaction, zoning out to the hum of the scanner and the faint hint of mildew.

From the minute he entered the classroom, he knew he'd made a mistake. The last thing he wanted was to talk to anyone, let alone a room full of apathetic and judgmental 19-year-olds. There had been a point when Mercer had convinced himself that he enjoyed these intermittent forays into teaching. After a day of scanning books by himself, it was nice to talk about the importance of research. He knew a great deal about how to use the library's catalog and was able to articulate all the ways that students could utilize the university's resources to improve their essays. Understood the arbitrary and sometimes downright stupid nuances of citing in bulky MLA, idiotic APA, and pretentious Chicago. "It sounds good for you," Alejandra had told him. "Maybe they'll eventually give you your own class."

He introduced himself without looking any of them in the eyes and sped through the slides on credible sources. He knew he was boring, probably even unhelpful, but he didn't care.

A girl in the front row raised her hand. "Can you go back to the last slide? The one about the digital catalogs."

He flipped back to the slide and the girl started jotting down notes. A kid in a backward Phillies hat raised his hand. "When she's done, can we go back to the sample Works Cited page? I missed it."

As he waited for the girl to finish writing, Mercer felt the need to fill the silence. "I'm usually a little more engaged. I apologize. I've been a bit all over the place today. Last two days, actually."

No one spoke. For the first time in his career, all of the students were paying attention to him.

He took a deep breath and finally felt at ease. He should explain himself, he thought. They should know that there's more to life than their upcoming paper. They should know that adult life is filled with unpredictable bouts of confusion and despair.

"My wife disappeared the other night," he said. "A note was left behind, but I don't believe it's her. It just doesn't make sense." He shifted uncomfortably behind the podium and felt the back of his retainer with the tip of his tongue. “So, yeah, I’m a little lost.”

The kid in the Phillies hat raised his hand again. Mercer braced himself for an emotional question, one that would cut deep. He knew he needed to be honest with him, even if it hurt.

“Can you go back to that Works Cited slide now?”

16.

Mercer and his father only spoke about Alejandra disappearing on the day it happened.

"You going to look for her?" he asked Mercer. He was in the yard at the family home across the river, staring at the fire pit, and talking through a Bluetooth earpiece.

Mercer was in his rowhome, the one that technically belonged to him and Alejandra. "The letter made it pretty clear I should leave her alone."

"What'd it say?"

"It said: 'please leave me alone while I figure this out.'"

"What's 'this'?"

"I don't know. I don't know anything. I'm worried she's in trouble."

"That letter doesn't even sound like her. I mean, right? Am I wrong here? That sound like her to you?"

"I don't know. I don't know how to begin understanding this."

"Maybe she didn't write that letter. Maybe she was abducted." He said this like it was encouraging. "Hey: that's a real possibility."

Five minutes later, they already seemed determined to avoid it. "I'm not trying to bog you down. If you need to talk, I'm here," his dad said. "But I also know sometimes it's best not to talk about the hard stuff."

So, they stayed away from it and got onto more important

matters, like how much he hated his neighbor, Alan. “He was out in his yard, trying to fix that piece of shit four-wheeler that he’s had up on cinderblocks for a decade. You know which one I’m talking about.”

“Yeah.”

“And he’s just *banging* it with a hammer. I mean, just *wailing* on it. As if that’s going to magically resuscitate this thing. This town gets worse by the day. I’m literally surrounded by retards.”

“Dad, Jesus.”

“What?”

“Just...*retards*.”

“It means ‘slow.’ I can’t say someone’s ‘slow’ now?”

“Say ‘slow’ then. And even that...”

“Oh, for Christ’s sake, Mercer, it’s a goddamn word. It’s a medical term. Doctors still use it. As in: ‘the boy was born with generalized mental retardation.’”

Mercer was relieved this was over the phone. It was easier to correct his dad without having to look him in the eyes. “Sure.”

“Right. Now you’re pissed. You think I’m insensitive or something. Fine. Be mad. Anyway, the point of my story was that Alan was in his backyard, taking his anger out on an inanimate object. And he looked fucking retarded.”

17.

Mercer's father lived in National Park, a small town on the banks of the Delaware River that was home to no National Parks. Instead, there was a small pizza place that housed hordes of teenagers on Friday nights, some of whom ordered pizza. There was a windowless V.F.W. hall that held karaoke on Tuesdays and had $7 buckets of Rolling Rocks on Thursdays, which is a pretty good deal if you do the math.

The town was named in 1902, 14 years before the National Park system was created, to commemorate a Revolutionary War battle fought on the banks of the Delaware River. There are concrete historical markers and illustrated placards there today, though no one seems to acknowledge them. Most people who visit the park have been there so many times that they've forgotten its history. Rather than soldiers, it's now usually populated by a handful of retired husbands desperate for routine, idling in their cars and reading the *Courier-Post* while they sip burnt Wawa coffee. Sometimes, they acknowledge each other with half-hearted waves, but they never exchange words.

On a field trip to the battlefield in third grade, Mercer listened as his teacher explained that the town was once a vacation destination for Protestant families. She described the scene in detail as she gestured to the empty waterfront. "Hundreds of families would flock to the beaches," she'd said. "And their one-room cottages were just a bit further back in the man-made dunes. The water was so clean that children spent their afternoons catching fish by hand." Even then, back when he didn't have to try too hard to trigger his imagination, he'd struggled to picture such an idyllic slice of Americana in his backyard.

18.

When Evan left rehab, he moved back in with his parents. After a week, his dad invited him to work at Moore Tech, the software consulting company he'd started 30 years earlier out of the family home.

"I don't know much about computers," Evan told him. "That was always Mercer's thing."

"I didn't know anything at the start either. But I learned."

"Clients won't pay to watch me learn."

"Clients don't know anything. That's why they come to us."

"I don't even know Excel, Dad."

"You learn their software. You study it like anything else. And then," he said, smiling, "we're just teaching them how to keep time on their own watches."

The number of people who left rehab clean and then fell back off the wagon was astronomical. Evan's father knew his son needed something stable, but he knew he also needed something impressive—a title that deserved to stand beside his name.

"You're not an addict," his dad told him once when the family was visiting him in rehab. "You're Evan Moore."

The others in the program had objectively worse stories—they'd totaled cars, hit wives, lost kids. Most of them were older, finally coming to Jesus after decades of fucking up. They all looked exhausted, no matter the time of day. A few of them took to Evan, warning him about the mistakes they'd made, reminding him he still had a long road in front of him.

Evan's rock bottom was what the other guys had been doing before it had all gone to shit. Considering that, he rarely piped up during meetings. What was he going to say? "I drank myself into a stupor, but my family still loved me"? He imagined the forced applause that would follow and decided he could offer more by listening, by just showing up.

For a while, he felt guilty for being so fortunate. But the more he sat through those meetings, the more he realized the difference wasn't in drama but in stakes. To really lose something, you needed to possess it in the first place.

19.

The fact that Evan Moore's new life started at a church-sponsored sober BBQ would've been unbearably depressing if the details of his previous one hadn't been far bleaker. It was a schedule that was never pre-ordained but always felt inevitable.

SUNDAYS - THURSDAYS	FRIDAYS	SATURDAYS	EVERY MORNING
shooting pool at ERA and drinking shots of well whiskey with Aaron, the unbathed conspiracy-theory spouting bar back	blacking out in the college bars on Market Street, ignoring the fraternity brothers who glared at him like he'd glared at the local drunks a decade earlier	drinking a twelve of rust-flavored Natural Ice and staring blankly at the fire pit in his parents' backyard in National Park	tasting hot acid, swallowing fistfuls of Excedrin, and throwing piss-stained sheets in the washing machine (though not always in that order)

So, a church BBQ, for all its painfully stilted conversations and overexcited Eucharistic ministers, was not so bad. At the least, he thought, it would've made his Mom happy.

His sponsor had been the one pushing it. "They reached out, so it's only polite. They don't charge us for meetings, you know," he'd said at the end of one meeting. Despite the insistence, Evan was still determined to avoid it and fabricated a story about helping his dad with repairs on the weekend house. "Can't," he'd told his sponsor, "I'm laying a brick walkway." He'd hoped that the specificity of the lie made it sound more believable, but the guy called bullshit, which, Evan supposed, was proof he was a good sponsor.

"If you allow yourself to have a good time, you might be surprised," he'd told Evan. "Or you can spend another Saturday jerking off in your parents' bathroom. But I think you know how that one ends."

Colleen was the first person from the church he met. Evan could tell from her face that she wasn't much older than him even though she dressed like a retiree at a craft fair. Her bright pastel top and long, denim skirt seemed like they were trying to spite the July humidity. She was fidgety in conversation—clearly uncomfortable, yet incapable of stopping herself from talking. She referenced saints from the fifth century like they were members of her extended family and insisted that Evan would make a great adult leader for the youth group's annual weekend retreat.

"Have you worked with kids before?" she asked.

"I worked as a camp counselor in high school."

"I knew I sensed something in there," she said and grinned.

Evan didn't tell her that he'd been fired in the first week after the camp director found eight Poland Spring bottles of vodka under his bed. In the past he would've been sure to include this detail, hoping to spoil someone like Colleen's optimism with just a little bit of reality. But he didn't want to do that—he didn't want Colleen to know that he'd been that way. He didn't want her to know a lot of things.

"So, you guys are in the rectory every Monday, right?"

Evan nodded and took a sip from his fruit punch. Years earlier, the anxiety of talking to a woman would've been gradually muted by the contents of his cup. Now, it just stained his lips.

"How many days sober are you?" The question lingered in the air for a beat before Colleen let out a nervous laugh. "I'm sorry—that's incredibly personal? You *don't* need to answer that. I'm rude? Incredibly rude. Please don't answer that."

"462," Evan said, though he was uncertain if that was the exact number. He kept track by months, worried that counting every day was too generous. Those guys who kept calendars, who crossed out every day they hadn't given in, always seemed to be the ones who fell off the hardest.

"462. Tremendous," she said and toasted him with her cup. "I don't drink either. Never have. Not even communion wine. I just—I don't know. It doesn't sound appealing when you put it on paper?"

He had no idea what she was talking about. "Totally," he said. "It's much clearer to me now. With some perspective."

"Like, a liquid that makes you loud and careless. And shortens your life. And causes dependency. I mean—I've never understood it. My college roommate, my freshman year roommate, she rushed a sorority. Every night for a month she'd come back, tipsy, spitting up on her shirt, slurring her words. I guess she enjoyed it? She looked miserable." Evan didn't know if he was supposed to interject. He couldn't recall a question. "I'm sorry. I'm rambling."

"No, no, it's fine. Really."

"I do this. Gah!" She pointed to her mouth. "Word vomit."

"Nothing to apologize for," Evan said. "I like listening."

She smiled. "You seem like an interesting person."

"I used to be," he said. "But I'm trying to be better."

20.

Most days, staying sober was surprisingly easy. His sponsor would text him every afternoon, just to check in. "All good?"

Most days, Evan would just reply with a thumbs-up emoji. He knew the guy didn't believe him and he didn't blame him. Getting sober wasn't supposed to be easy. According to the program, Evan was still an alcoholic and would always be one. What Evan wanted to tell his sponsor was that he *did* still want to drink. Badly. He wanted the warmth that came with a fourth beer. He wanted the tingling lips that came with a sip of neat bourbon. He wanted to have a drink with his brother because he knew having something to focus on during the long silences would help bridge the distance between them.

It wasn't mental fortitude that stopped him from falling off the wagon, like his dad assumed. It wasn't his rediscovered faith, either, though Colleen would argue otherwise. More than anything, it was a deep, palpable shame.

People at the meetings always talked about letting go of shame, that they were individuals, complex and unique people, who weren't defined by one span of time. They were still actualizing; they were in the process of becoming their best selves. Evan clapped along with everyone else at the ends of these speeches, but secretly he couldn't ignore the truth: the people who used those words, who were so quick to talk about absolving themselves of any and all blame, were always the first ones to fall back down.

The new world said shame was something to work through, to move beyond. But Evan wasn't so sure. Maybe shame wasn't such a bad thing. Maybe shame was keeping him alive.

21.

It was their third date when Colleen suggested Evan sit down with Father Brad. "He's a good ear," she said. "I know a lot of guys in the parish talk to him. It's 'spiritual guidance,' but he lets you define the 'spiritual' part."

Brad wasn't like the other priests at St. Catherine's. He hated wearing the collar, for one. "It puts people off," he told Evan. "And it's hot as hell." Unless he was on the altar, he preferred long cargo shorts and an oversized button-up with the sleeves rolled to his elbows.

And he didn't like to call their sessions "counseling" or "therapy," even though, as he made it clear to Evan, he was licensed to call it either of those things if he wanted. "I look at it as a conversation," he said in their first meeting.

Evan knew this was a lame trick to try and connect, one that every young-ish priest he'd ever met had attempted. During mandatory confession in grade school, his Monsignor had told him to "forget the sins and tell me about the Sixers." The 20-something campus minister at his high school had asked him if he liked any "conscious hip-hop artists."

In general, he'd always found the approach to be shamelessly transparent and unbearably dorky. That's why he was surprised when he found himself willing to excuse Father Brad's spin on it.

"He seems really happy," Evan told Colleen. "Where do you think that comes from?"

22.

It was Father Brad who suggested the trip to the Pine Barrens.

"You mentioned last week you were concerned about your brother."

"Still am."

"How'd your conversation with him go?"

Evan thought back to the tense look in Mercer's eyes. "I spoke, but I don't know that he heard me."

"Do you have plans for the Fourth?"

The question surprised him. "I don't think so. I usually watch the fireworks from the park," he said. The year before had been the first time since sixth grade that he'd done it sober. It'd been him and his dad in camping chairs, grilling hot dogs and complaining about the Phillies' shitty bullpen. When the explosions started, Evan stared up at the sky in awe. At the grand finale, he'd looked around at the other families scattered across the lawn and realized the only other children with their parents were all under ten years old.

"Doesn't your dad have a place down the shore?"

The cabin was tucked away in Ong's Hat, a section of the Pine Barrens that looked more like Alabama than New Jersey. "It's on the way."

"Do you see what I'm getting at?"

Evan nodded, though he had no idea.

"Might be good for Mercer to get away—spend some time

with you and your dad. A little bit of male bonding."

Evan didn't know the last time the three of them had spent more than a meal together. He figured it had to have been years ago, in a rental down the shore, with their Mom. Back when she was still around.

On his drive home, when he proposed the trip to Mercer over the phone, he didn't mention that memory. All he said was, "I thought it might be fun."

23.

At work, Mercer tried to keep his phone face down on his desk. He'd read somewhere that it made the thing less alluring; it'd been proven and published in a psychological or sociological journal, though he couldn't recall which one. Not that he could name any psychological or sociological journals and not that he would've been able to verify any scientific article if it came across his desk. Still: the point was that the phone's appeal was minimized just by being turned over. The psychologists/sociologists had proven it, empirically.

So, as he scanned books in the back room, he kept his phone face down on his desk, though whenever it buzzed he still couldn't help turning it over, hoping to see Alejandra's name flashing across the screen.

That never came. Instead, there were *New York Times* alerts about the election, even though voting was still months away. Sometimes there were warnings that a child had been kidnapped 100 miles away from the city. Mercer couldn't be positive, but he was almost certain they always identified the same Nissan Altima.

The morning after his brother proposed the trip to the Pine Barrens, the phone buzzed, and Mercer once again turned it over. This time it was a group text filled with unrecognizable South Jersey numbers.

Deacon Greg heading back in for checkup.

Please keep him in your prayers.

Mercer didn't know Deacon Greg and couldn't understand how he'd wound up in a group chat about him. As he continued staring at the screen, the replies started streaming in.

Will add him to my list

thank you for update

It had to have been Evan. Or Colleen. Likely Colleen via Evan. Mercer felt his plastic retainer with his tongue and began typing.

10 Hail Mary's coming right up! Who's with me?!

He placed the phone face down on the desk and smiled. A minute later there was another buzz.

That's the spirit!

24.

On the way home, acrid black smoke began billowing from the hood of Mercer's car. He called AAA and waited, wishing he could do something other than stare at his wreck.

"How did this happen?" he asked the tow driver.

"I don't know. It's your car. Do you take good care of it?"

"I don't know. I thought I did. I just had it inspected."

The tow driver shrugged. "Bad luck, I guess. Someone upstairs out to get you."

"You think it's salvageable?"

"I just tow. That's a question for the mechanic."

"But in your experience, if you've seen something like this before...you thinking a few hundred? A few thousand?"

"Like I said, I don't really know."

Mercer's phone buzzed in his pocket. "Is that because you don't know, or your job doesn't allow you to speculate?"

"All I've seen is black smoke coming from your car. If you want me to speculate, I'd say you're fucked."

Another buzz in the pocket. He thought to ask if it might be the carburetor but wasn't sure if he knew the difference between that and the transmission. How was it possible that he'd forced himself to read the modernists in college, yet he'd never had the discipline to read his owner's manual?

Mercer imagined himself through the tow driver's eyes—a grown man with plastic teeth in slim khakis and a tucked-in dress shirt, so utterly helpless that he needed another man to explain the depths of his utter helplessness.

When they arrived at the mechanic's, Mercer went into the bathroom and checked the voicemail from the missed call. It was Detective Williams, informing him that his wife Alejandra Bianchi Moore was safe. She was out of town, staying with some friends. "And I know you had your doubts, but she confirmed the letter was written by her," she said. Mercer felt his face grow hot with embarrassment as the detective mentioned details about the case being closed. It all started to run together until he heard the words "restraining order."

"She did not mention the need for one, but I suggested if you violated the requests in her letter then she should call me directly."

This was not how Mercer imagined things unfolding. Since Alejandra had disappeared, he'd had several daydreams about how it would all end. Even though the details of each one differed, the resolution was mostly the same.

DAYDREAM #	1	2	3
TIME OF DAY	Early morning, usually on the morning commute	Late afternoon	Late at night, while trying to fall asleep
RESOLUTION	She runs into his arms; fireworks illuminate the night sky behind them	He punches a greasy, basement dwelling, school-shooter/incel type and, in turn, frees her from knife-point	She knocks on the front door of their house, tears in her eyes, and says, "please forgive me" over and over and over again

He had not pictured:

REALITY
1. Being on the toilet 2. Feeling worse than when he'd read her initial letter 3. Someone banging on the door, telling him to "hurry up in there"

25.

Alejandra's sister Maria hadn't returned any of Mercer's ten phone calls. It wasn't hard to imagine her pressing "Decline" every time his name appeared or deleting each of his emotionally charged voicemails without so much as reading the first line of the transcription. Yet it also wasn't hard to imagine her conflicted—to picture her writing long, sympathetic texts to him before erasing them, to imagine her telling her husband Tom that Mercer was the real victim here, to see her persuading Alejandra to move beyond whatever quarter-life crisis she'd imagined and head back home. It really wasn't hard to imagine *any* of it, Mercer realized. It was all a matter of perspective.

Maria and Tom lived just a few blocks away, so after he returned home from the mechanic's, Mercer poured a beer into a coffee mug and started walking. Tom was sitting on the stoop in his socks and sandals, staring at his phone. Above their door was a SOLD sign featuring the face of their realtor, a thumb of a man with slicked black hair and a confident stare. Alejandra had told Mercer that her sister was moving to the suburbs, but he couldn't remember the specifics. It was Blue Bell, or Flourtown, or one of the other many sprawls with a ridiculous name.

"Finally getting out of the city, huh?" Mercer asked, pointing to the sign.

Tom's body jerked, surprised to find him there. "Jesus, Mercer. You scared me."

"Just on an evening stroll. And I guess I need to congratulate you. Where you guys headed?"

Tom looked horrified. "This is a bad idea." He was nearly whispering.

"I swear I didn't expect to run into you. Honest. I actually forgot you guys were on this block. Maybe my brain was on autopilot." Mercer took a sip from his mug. The beer flowed into his plastic retainers and soaked his naked teeth.

Tom looked over his shoulder before speaking. "Listen, if you need someone to talk to, I'm here for you. Outside of all of this, you're my friend." Over the years, the two of them had spent many hours at Bianchi family dinners and second cousins' birthday parties, drinking light beer and trying to pass the hours by pretending to be invested in whatever game happened to be on the nearest television. Mercer didn't know what to call it, exactly, but he wasn't sure it was a friendship. "We can talk. It just *can't* be here," Tom said.

"Just get Maria, Tom."

"You should go home."

"Just get your wife, Tom."

Maria swung the door open and scowled. Mercer wondered how long she'd been waiting there, listening in on their conversation. She was wearing her PENN ALUMNA crewneck even though the July humidity was sweltering. At family dinners, Mercer and Alejandra had made a habit out of secretly counting the number of times Maria namedropped Penn. With every infraction, they made eyes and tried desperately to stifle their laughter.

"You're shitting me, right?" Maria said. "What part of 'don't contact my family' do you not understand?"

"You read the letter?"

"Of course, I read the letter. I'm her sister."

Mercer took another sip from the mug. It was already lukewarm.

"Missing Persons called my mom this morning, asking her if she knew the whereabouts of her daughter. She was destroyed. Do you understand what I'm saying, Mercer?" She paused, catching her breath. "You sent my family into a fucking panic this morning, all because you can't accept some very simple requests."

Mercer felt his face growing hot. He knew it would be best to walk away without saying another word, but he couldn't swallow the fact that Maria—the Maria who Alejandra had complained about so many times, the Maria who'd spent an entire Matron of Honor toast talking about herself—was now Alejandra's noble protector. "My wife disappears without any reason. I try to get some answers and suddenly I'm the bad guy?"

"She asked you to give her some space and you act like it's this absolute impossibility."

"A letter like that? Out of nowhere? That's alarming. That's a red flag." He wanted to be as stoic as the smirking realtor from their SOLD sign, but he could feel his hand beginning to shake. "I'm concerned, Maria. I'm concerned for my wife."

She stared at him, allowing the silence to sit in the humid air for a few beats. "You know, I used to think you were smart. And considerate. I used to at least think you were considerate. But you know what, Mercer? You're not. You're arrogant. And you're delusional. And I want you off my property."

He looked at the ground and then back at her. "I'm in a public street."

"You contact me, my sister, my parents, our cousins, anyone, and *I'm* filing a restraining order. You hear me?"

"So, I'm not supposed to contact anyone? *Anyone*, Maria?"

"I want you to say 'yes,' you dense motherfucker."

Rather than giving in, Mercer downed the rest of his mug and burped. Maria slammed the door and Tom suddenly stood up from the stoop. He shifted his feet, widening his stance to match the length of the doorframe. He crossed his arms and looked down at Mercer. Like he was protecting the house. Like Mercer was some kind of unhinged lunatic.

"Is this a joke, Tom?"

Tom shook his head. "Sorry, buddy. Maria doesn't really like jokes."

Part 2: Ong's Hat

1.

Lake Moore was in the driveway, melting into his Kelly green Eagles chair. He stared at the house, a modest two-bedroom rancher, and tried to imagine what it could look like if he dedicated time—real time—to fixing it up. It would take at least a summer, permits with the township, and about twenty grand. The summer he had; the other details would work themselves out.

Here was a sight to behold, he thought: a 72-year-old, greying man treating a chair like a hammock. There was a chance a nosy neighbor might take him for dead. There was a chance they might do something stupid like call an ambulance. So, he tried to straighten up, hoping it might throw off any overly concerned onlookers. He'd only had a single edible, but he felt like he was wearing the chair. It'd travel with him if he decided to walk to the backyard and survey the ground for a deck. Not that he was actually going to do that. He wasn't sure he could stand, for one thing.

It'd been just one of the gummies, one of the 5mg guys that looked like peaches but for some reason tasted like grapes. He'd convinced himself that he'd developed a bit of a tolerance, but this particular peach had caught him off guard. One minute he was staring at the door to the house, imagining it with a slightly lighter shade of brown, picturing it on some shining stainless hinges, and then: *Woah.*

How was it possible that this batch was stronger than the

last if they all came from the same lab in Vineland? Wasn't the benefit of medical weed that they'd ironed out all of the unpredictable aspects from back in the day? What if he took one more?

He'd stopped smoking after they had Evan. And, for a long time, he hadn't missed it. It wasn't until an old friend, someone from his previous life, recommended he get a medical card after Brigid passed.

"You don't even need to actually see a doctor. You just call this guy, tell him you can't sleep, and he'll mail you a card."

"Sounds like bullshit," Lake had said.

"It *is* bullshit. But you'll finally get some sleep."

He could sometimes go a full day without thinking about her, but he always remembered when he put his head down on the pillow and didn't find her there. It was dumb, he thought, reducing her to just a physical presence, but it's what had happened.

And his friend was right: the medical card made things better. Or, at least, it made things easier. A glass of bourbon and one of the peach gummies usually knocked him out cold. So maybe it wasn't bullshit. Maybe it *was* medicinal. It was just an added bonus that, in addition to its medicinal purposes, he could take one with his coffee and fully appreciate a Saturday morning.

He'd purchased the house six months earlier. The boys laughed when he told them. No one bought vacation homes in the Pine Barrens. Growing up he'd heard that it was the home of the Jersey Devil, of meth heads and inbreeds, of the NJ Chapter of the KKK. It'd always been a place he'd avoided—something to drive through, not towards.

But he'd received a call from an old client, a guy he hadn't seen in fifteen years, someone who hadn't even heard the news about Brigid. "I'm selling my place and thought of you," he'd said. Lake didn't ask why. A lifetime ago he would've called it cosmic, a concrete example of kismet, but now he just considered it dumb luck. A good opportunity.

It wasn't much. It was in Communion, a town up by Ong's Hat Road with a population so small that it didn't even have its own zip code. The bedrooms of the cabin were small, and the kitchen hadn't been updated since the early 60s, but it had a wood-burning stove that calmed him in a way he'd never known. And the plot—four wooded acres overrun with towering pines—was a welcome contrast to the suburban squares of National Park.

And, yeah, sometimes when he was really high it was all a bit too much, all the nothing, but during the day it was a miracle; the silence slowed time, presenting the day as an opportunity void of everyone else's interjections.

When the old client was pitching the place to Lake over the phone, he'd said, "If you wanted, you could spend a lifetime up here without seeing a soul."

Lake hadn't said it out loud, but that had been the selling point.

2.

In the first 31 minutes of the ride to their dad's cabin, Evan and Mercer cycled through all of their standard topics of conversation.

WORK

"It's just grown mind-numbing," Mercer said.

"You know Moore Tech can always bring you on."

"I'm not interested in teaching the Silent Generation to tweet."

Evan forced a laugh. "It's really about learning the language of software."

"Sounds mind-numbing."

SPORTS

"I only watch when Dad invites me over. I can't even name five players at this point."

"You know more than you think," Evan said. "Velasquez. Galvis. Howard."

"Ryan Howard? He's still playing?"

"He's still on the team, yeah."

"How old is he?"

"36."

"Shouldn't he have retired by now? He can't possibly need more money."

"Maybe he doesn't know what else to do."

"Go on permanent vacation. Coach Little League. Sleep."

"I don't know if it's that easy for some people."

"I've wanted to retire since I started working."

THE NEWS

"She's favored by something like 90%. It's a given," Mercer said. "Even the G.O.P. can't unite behind him."

"But that's probability. That 10% could still happen." Evan had read a headline that morning that had said those exact words. He was hoping his brother wouldn't ask him to elaborate. "It's just not as probable."

"But *won't* happen."

"Most likely won't."

"Do you know anyone who's voting for him?"

Evan shrugged. He knew most of the people involved with the church only voted for candidates vocally opposed to abortion, but he wondered if this time might be different. The night before, Colleen had mentioned how disappointed she was that there were two terrible candidates. "It's choosing the lesser of two evils," she had said, but he didn't have the nerve to ask her to elaborate.

THEIR FATHER

"Is dad voting for him?"

"No idea."

"You haven't had any conversations about it?"

"None. I've gone out of my way to avoid it."

Mercer recalled the way his dad spoke about race ("I don't care if someone's black, white, yellow…"), the op-ed he'd written to the *Courier Post* decrying rising property taxes, the subtle but undeniably surprised look in his eyes when he mentioned he'd started seeing someone named Alejandra. "But you think there's a shot," he told his brother.

"Always a shot. Even if it's only 10%."

It was in minute 32 that it all came to a halt. There was more to discuss, but with only 20 miles of road remaining, they both tacitly agreed that it would all have to wait for another time. Instead, they stared at pine trees and hand-scrawled NO TRESPASSING signs, listening in silence to the fading signal of the city's NPR affiliate.

3.

They stopped for lunch at Olga's, a diner that advertised 26 different kinds of hamburgers, one for every letter of the alphabet. It sat on a busy traffic circle that offered drivers passage into every corner of the state, something the waitress was quick to point out. "We get people from all over—Delran, Tuckerton, Salem."

"Exotic," Mercer said, and his brother glared at him.

They had been here before, a decade earlier. Mercer had just turned 17, which meant Evan was 18 and a half. "Irish twins," their aunt used to say when they were younger, a phrase Mercer didn't properly understand until long after his mother had stopped talking to her sister.

Evan was the one with the friends, guys who would assemble in the backyard every summer night, brainstorming about meeting up with girls and buying beer. Good nights were when both happened. Good nights were very rare.

When they wanted to escape the limits of National Park, Evan called Mercer out to the yard and threw him the keys to their parents' minivan. They wanted to go to the Shore. They wanted to find the Atco Ghost, to finally try Taylor Ham. The requests always began like that—there was never a particular destination so much as an idea.

That night, they wanted to drive to the Pine Barrens.

"Why?" Mercer asked, as if he was considering not driving.

"Because this town sucks and Conor read about some shit in *Weird NJ.* Who cares?"

On the drive, Evan and his friends passed around bottles of Poland Spring filled with the clear stuff from Greg Carmody's parents' liquor cabinet. Conor babbled on about Mary Leeds, the mother who cursed her 13th child and inadvertently spawned the Jersey Devil, about the overwhelming evidence proving the existence of a Satanic church on Indian Cabin Road, about the horde of child molesters who stalked the woods and tempted kids with Dr. Pepper.

Mercer thought Conor was a gullible moron, but he stayed quiet. He was just happy Evan had brought him along. He knew the main reason he'd been invited wasn't because he was good company, but because they needed a chauffeur to escort their drunk asses. Still, he thought, they could've forced any of their younger brothers to DD and they'd chosen him.

By the time they got to the Pines, Conor was hammered and incapable of providing coherent directions. Instead of investigating any particular oddity, they drove down narrow sand roads and stared off into the overpowering darkness of the summer night. Eventually, someone said they were hungry, and someone else said pancakes would hit the spot, and soon enough they were at Olga's, staring down the same spiral-bound menus that Evan and Mercer would stare down ten years later.

Evan had possessed such an easy charm back then—he was the ringleader of that gang of high-achieving potheads and

Honors Society drunks. Mercer never joined their summer meetings in the backyard unless he was invited, but he often spied on the proceedings from his bedroom window, marveling at the way everyone quieted down when his brother spoke and the genuine laughter that broke out every time he cracked a joke. Back then, Evan possessed a shit-eating grin he'd flash at parents, teachers, and friends alike. People wanted to be close to him—even if he was an asshole, even if he was a problem, even if he was bringing them down. Their mom had described it as an "electric personality." One of Mercer's teachers was a bit more precise: "Your brother is the most lovable scoundrel in the world."

There was so much that came after: the expulsion from college, the failed stint at rehab, the first D.U.I., the missing money, the second D.U.I., the rumors of pills. There was more that Mercer was sure he was forgetting, details he'd discarded when he'd run out of emotional bandwidth.

He knew that Evan would've killed himself if he hadn't cleaned up. He knew that. But sometimes, at moments like that one, as he struggled to find something to say to his brother at a shitty roadside diner in the Pines, he wondered why Evan couldn't have held onto just a little of the electricity.

4.

This isn't the only story about the Pine Barrens. It's not even clear if this is a story about the Pine Barrens, is it? No, I don't know that it is. Clear, I mean.

It's the kind of setting that begs for mythology. These woods are filled with stories. Here's one.

Jacob Ong was a regular at the dances they held near Lebanon Lake back in the late 1700s. He was known to wear a silk top hat, an accessory that was said to make him look a full foot taller. You can imagine that in the 18th century this drew the attention of every room he entered. I suppose some women were into that kind of thing. I imagine the guys rolled their eyes, like, "here comes Ong and that fucking *hat* again."

One day, a woman named Sara heard her friends talking about the man with the hat. She thought he sounded so mysterious and urbane, so unlike everything she'd ever known. She'd never been certain of anything in her life, but she knew she needed to meet this Jacob Ong.

Sara arrived early to the next week's dance, waiting for the man she'd dreamt about. When she finally spotted him, she crossed the room, grabbed him by the hands, and brought him out to the dance floor. She leaned against his body and felt his natural heat. This is the one, she thought. This is the man I've always wanted.

Ong said he needed to run to the outhouse, but that he'd be right back. "Don't go finding someone else," he told her. She laughed. It was an absurd idea.

An hour passed, and Sara grew worried. Something must've happened to Jacob. She walked out of the hall and towards the outhouse. That was where she found Ong leaning up against a tree, whispering into the ear of some other woman.

Sara slapped the girl. The people who'd been standing around gasped. It even surprised Sara—she'd never slapped anyone in her life. Still, she was filled with a rage that had pushed her beyond the recommendations of her conscience. She grabbed the silk hat from Ong's head, threw it down to the ground, and stomped on it until it was stained and tattered.

Both women stormed off in opposite directions, leaving Ong alone with his ruined hat. He felt like he had lost his name: no one would recognize him from across the room again. He didn't even consider the silk tatters worth saving. He tossed the thing as high as he could, sending it to the upper reaches of the tree he'd been leaning against. People say it stayed there for decades, creating a rare landmark in the middle of the wild, repetitive, disorienting Pines.

But that's impossible, right? You don't have to answer. I know it is. That hasn't stopped centuries of people from telling the story. That didn't stop people from naming the town settled at the alleged tree "Ong's Hat."

Who cares if it's true? It'll make you look at that pine tree differently.

I do wonder about Sara, though. Every version of the story ends with Jacob throwing the hat in the air, but no version I've read ever explains what came of her. No one ever explains if she ever realized that Jacob wasn't the man of her dreams. No one ever explains if she ever realized she needed to stop putting so much stock in dreams.

5.

The inside of their father's cabin was all shades of amber and brown, its walls lined with random, rusted items he'd picked up from Craigslist. When Evan walked through the door and set down his bag, he felt like he'd crawled into a stranger's shed.

"Not too shabby, huh?" Lake said, standing in the kitchen. "Needs some polishing, but I like the feel." He wanted to show them his grand plans for the cabin, so he took them to the back lot and pointed at what he imagined. "Wooden platform. Orchestra seating," he said.

"So, a deck," Mercer said. "Gonna be difficult considering the ground isn't even close to level." He knelt down and thumbed the mossy ground like he knew what he was doing. "Has someone surveyed this for you? You need to get a professional, so this thing doesn't sink in."

"You're overthinking this," Lake said. "You've got to dream a little before you plan. Now, listen. I mean, really: *listen.* I want you to hear the woods a little bit so you can see what I mean by orchestra seating."

"Dad," Mercer said, "are you stoned?"

"It's a joke. Lighten up." He put a hand on Mercer's shoulder and massaged it. "But, yeah, I had a pretty decent edible with breakfast." He took a deep breath and offered a smile that showed just about every one of his teeth. "Is that a crime?"

Lake grilled hot dogs and corn for dinner, explaining that he still hadn't gotten the hang of shopping for one. "I don't have the foresight for that shit. And I always do it hungry, which means I'm practically braindead, which means I end up with dry pasta and potato chips." The boys told him not to worry, but he still felt uneasy. "There's a tub of coleslaw in the fridge if you end up needing something more," he said. "Store-bought, but pretty good."

The three of them sat in plastic chairs on the back lawn with paper plates on their laps and watched as the lightning bugs began to show off.

"I'm glad you boys could make it down here to spend some time with your dad," Lake said. "Sincerely."

"Thanks for having us," Evan said. Mercer nodded along with his brother, his mouth full of charred hot dogs.

"While you're here, I was thinking maybe you could help me out with the backyard. Can't do it by myself and don't want to pay some contractor who'd rip me off just to fuck it up."

Mercer didn't have any plans beyond sneaking a few of his dad's edibles, but he suddenly felt inconvenienced. "Have you ever built a deck? I told you that ground isn't level. You can't just mess around with this stuff."

"You're the pro now? Didn't realize you were in the trades."

"I'm just saying."

"I remodeled the Magnolia house by myself before you were born." Lake took a sip from his beer. "*Just saying.*"

Evan felt the tension budding in his chest. "You've got all the materials and everything?"

"Lumber yard offered to drop off everything we need by 8 a.m. We'll be done by the afternoon." He slapped Mercer's arm. "You might learn something. A life skill! I won't even charge you."

"Is this why you invited us here? Free labor?"

"I didn't invite anyone here," he said without a smile. "But, hey, you're welcome for the hospitality anyways."

"Let's take a few steps back," Evan said. "Let's everybody just collect themselves for a minute."

6.

The first thing Lake did after buying the cabin was construct a fire pit in the front yard. It hadn't taken more than an hour: all it'd required was some easy digging, pouring a bit of sand, and piling a bunch of cinderblocks. No leveling required.

After dinner they assembled their chairs around his sagging creation, allowing the fire's hisses and crackles to fill the gaps in conversation. Every few minutes, Lake would jab at one of the logs, trying to make it flame up. Evan drank cans of pomegranate sparkling water, matching his brother's beers drink-for-drink. They talked about the weather and the mosquitos. Other than that, no one said much.

In their last meeting before the weekend, Father Brad had given Evan a deck of cards. "They're called Conversation Starters. In case of an emergency." Evan had shuffled through the deck, reading the one-sentence questions they posed.

CONVERSATION STARTERS!
What's the hardest you've ever laughed?
Follow up: who's the funniest person you know and why?

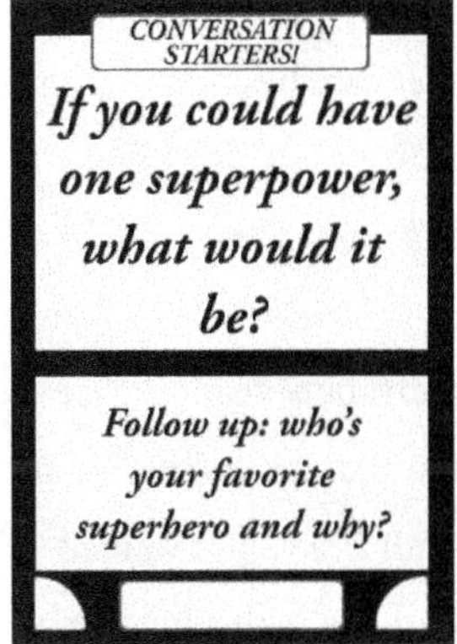

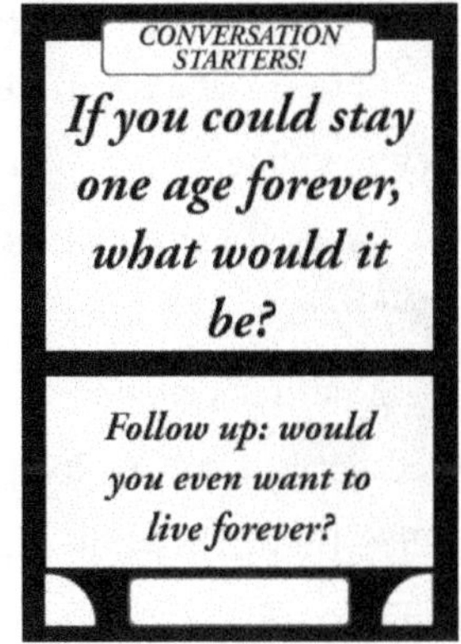

"I think you'll be surprised with the results," Father Brad had said. "These things kill on retreats."

In the middle of one of the longer silences, Evan reached for the cards in his pocket. He was sure that the two of them would laugh him off, but he decided that would be all right. If it cut through some of the tension, if it helped everyone open up a bit, that would be fine.

Before he could grab them, Lake spoke up. "You guys heard of Gary Johnson?"

Mercer laughed. "The Gary Johnson who's running for president?"

"I'm thinking of voting for him."

Mercer leaned forward in his chair, as if he hadn't heard his dad. "I can't tell if you're kidding."

"Why would I say it if I didn't mean it?"

"Guess I figured you were throwing your support behind the sociopath."

Lake scrunched his face. "He's a moron. C'mon."

"I read that a lot of Trump supporters are hesitant to admit they're voting for him because they know he's a racist."

"Sounds like a bullshit *New York Times* piece."

"*Politico*, but okay."

Evan remembered a similar conversation years earlier—McCain vs. Obama—though he'd been the one poking at his father. He was home from college on Fall Break and wanted to know why his parents were so uncomfortable with a black man running the country.

"It's got nothing to do with race," Lake had said.

"That's a lie and you know it," Evan had said. He remembered Mercer, then a junior in high school, wide-eyed as he watched the back-and-forth. Now Evan was the one hoping they could find some way on to a gentler topic.

"Johnson's running against Trump. As in if I'm voting for Johnson, I'm voting against Trump."

"'I'm thinking of Gary Johnson' might be another way of saying 'I'm voting for Trump.'"

"I'm not 'thinking of Gary Johnson.' I'm thinking of *voting* for him. At least give me the benefit of proper grammar. Jesus. If I was trying to avoid talking about Trump why would I bring this up?"

Evan cleared his throat. "Maybe we ditch politics? Maybe we make a rule: no talking politics at the cabin." The cards were in his hands now, and he shuffled through them anxiously, trying to find a question that they might not hate him for.

"We're all grown-ups. We can talk about these things. Right, Dad?"

"Depends on what you mean by talking. So far I've gathered that you understand my political opinions better than I do."

"Apparently Johnson's poll numbers are inflated specifically *because* people would rather say they're voting for him than say they're voting for Trump. That's all I'm saying."

"Well, I haven't been polled and I'm not voting for Trump. I'm not even sure I'm voting for Johnson. I'm *thinking* of voting for him."

"You can't bring yourself to vote for a woman?"

"So, let me get this straight. Because I don't like *her* I'm a sexist?"

"Never said you were a sexist. You're the one using that word."

"But you're implying it. You're winding your way around the point."

"I asked you a simple question. At least *I* thought it was simple."

Evan settled on *If you could live anywhere in the world, where would it be?* It wasn't perfect, but he knew nothing in the deck would be able to avoid the scorn of Moore family cynicism. "Maybe we should change the topic."

"No, let Dad explain his decision. You're *thinking* of voting for Gary Johnson because you're *not* a sexist. Anything else I'm missing?"

"Johnson's a reasonable man," Lake said, as if he was defending an old friend. "He's looking to slash taxes. He's not interested in the government interfering. He's run a business *and* a state." He looked around the night, as if there was someone else there who'd understand his frustration. "Can't believe I have to justify this to my own son."

"You think he really understands the intricacies of the economy? Of the Middle East?"

"Who the fuck does? Not me. And you might be too arrogant to admit it, but you don't either, Merce."

Mercer didn't know if the adrenaline pumping through his veins meant that he was terrified or invigorated. "Last time I checked, we weren't asking to be president."

"If you could live anywhere in the world, where would it be?" Evan said, cutting through. He took a sip from his seltzer and stared down at the card, unable to face the other two.

Mercer stormed off in search of another beer. Lake stood to turn over two of the flaming logs with his foot. "What kind of question is that?" he asked Evan. "I mean, shit. I just bought this place."

7.

Mercer took the couch, leaving the bedrooms for his dad and brother. The cabin was insufferable in the July humidity. He tried to ignore the puddle of sweat he felt forming between his back and the couch's thick paisley cushions, but it was impossible.

He tried distracting himself by scrolling through Instagram and Twitter, hoping a mutual friend might inadvertently reveal a clue about Alejandra's location. But all they had to offer were photos of lavish Airbnbs in faraway locations. Mercer swiped through every perfectly framed photo, hating the photographers for spending the long weekend in air-conditioned rooms, away from their families.

What he wanted was one more beer to put him over, even if it would guarantee a hangover in the morning. He Googled "beer" and found a brewery less than a mile from the cabin. He figured he was sober enough to drive, but he knew Evan would scold him if he found out he'd gotten behind the wheel after drinking. Mercer didn't want to give him the satisfaction, so he grabbed his shoes and started walking.

Sometimes when he couldn't sleep in the city he took walks around the block to calm his nerves. Something about the physical act ground the day's anxieties down into something more manageable. Alejandra had hated this habit, even though she was always asleep by the time he'd sneak out of the house. "Don't you think that's dangerous?" she'd said when he first told her. "I wouldn't even know if something happened to you." But it never felt dangerous. It never felt like anything, which was the point.

He walked to the end of the gravel driveway and followed the instructions on his phone. The darkness of the Pines was different than in South Philly: there was a streetlight every quarter mile or so but wandering through the black spaces between them was disorienting. He knew it was irrational, the stuff of horror movies and folklore rather than actual statistics, but he couldn't shake the fear that something was following him—an animal lurking in the trees or a serial killer on the loose. It was irrational but acknowledging its unlikeliness did nothing to eliminate it. For a second, he considered turning around and heading back to the cabin. Lying awake on the couch with one fewer beer was not ideal, though it was certainly better than being mutilated.

In the distance, he saw lights. *LENAPE BREWING COMPANY* was written in bold script below a Native American man in a headdress, his stoic face a tomato red. As Mercer walked towards the building, a voice from behind told him to stop. "You going in there?"

He turned to the voice and found a kid in cargo shorts and flip-flops, his face covered with acne and peach-fuzz. Mercer wondered if he'd snuck out past curfew. He wondered if kids still had curfews.

"You sure you want to support that place?"

"Just looking for a beer."

"The owner claims he's Lenape. One sixteenth or something. Talked about family documents and blood and everything. It's why he says the logo isn't racist."

Mercer looked back at the sign and realized he'd been focused on the bright light more than the actual image. "But he's not actually a Native American?"

The kid's face turned to pity for the grown man who struggled to grasp simple concepts. "It doesn't matter what he says he is." He pointed back at the sign. "That's a picture straight from a bounty."

Mercer really wanted the beer. He didn't know what to say. "I'm sorry. I don't think I know you. I'm just looking for a drink."

The kid held out his hand. "Nan."

"Nan," Mercer said. "Nan," he said again, trying to sound more confident.

"You expected Sitting Duck."

"I don't know. No, definitely not."

"Gambling Drunk."

Mercer laughed cautiously. He was almost positive he was being invited in on the joke. Almost.

In third grade, his class had spent a week learning about the Leni Lenape of New Jersey through a thin novel written by an archaeologist. The main character was a shipwrecked British boy who proved his worth to the Lenape by helping them farm the soil of the Pine Barrens. Mercer had pored over the book and its glossary of Lenape words, jealous of the shipwrecked kid. He'd underlined every geographic detail from the book, hoping that he could pinpoint the town where they'd eventually settled. If he remembered correctly, it was somewhere close to where he was now.

"Can we go see the tribe?" he'd asked his teacher after they'd finished the book.

"Unfortunately, they're no longer around," his teacher had told him. Mercer remembered asking why, but he didn't remember getting an answer.

Nan crouched down and grabbed two bricks from the grass. "Listen. I need your help." He approached Mercer with a brick in each hand, then stopped when he noticed Mercer's retainers. "Why are your teeth so shiny?"

"It's plastic. They're braces, technically."

"Fuck, man. Do they hurt?"

Mercer was confused by the tangent but was relieved that it suddenly felt like they were on the same team. "Early on they did, yeah. But then over time you just get used to it."

"Like anything, I guess."

"Like anything," Mercer said.

Nan studied his teeth for another minute before remembering why he was holding the bricks. "Alright, listen. We're going to throw these through their windows. If you think you can hit the logo, you should aim for that."

Mercer didn't take a brick. "That logo's awful and the guy sounds like a dick—"

"—the state doesn't even recognize our tribe, and this guy

has the nerve to *capitalize* on it—"

"—it sounds really bad. Really. I really sympathize. I do. But this is a bad idea." He took a breath and licked his top retainer. "A really bad idea."

The kid smiled. "You're right. It's going to infuriate them. What would make someone do such a thing? Why would someone toss a bright red stone through a bright red face?" Nan moved the bricks up and down a few times like he was lifting a barbell, then tossed one into the grass. "Listen. You don't need to do anything. All right? All I'm asking is that when they come looking for the culprit, tell them the truth."

Mercer attempted a smile, as if he finally understood. "But you'll be gone?"

"And you're going to tell them it was an Indian," he said, studying the brick that remained in his right palm. "They'll never believe it."

Before Mercer could object, Nan began pacing towards the building, his flip-flops squeaking with each step, before stepping in front of the window to evaluate the bullseye. The brick finally came to his ear and sat there for a beat, like it was telling him a secret. It was when Mercer turned to survey the parking lot, to see if anyone was on to them, that he realized he was an accessory. He was almost certain that was the term.

Mercer heard a wordless grunt and turned back to see the brick leave Nan's hand like a shotput aimed at the moon. By the time it'd reached the height of its arc, Nan was already running in the opposite direction, the squeaking of his flip-flops growing quieter with each step. When it hit, Mercer was still there, staring in amazement at the cascade of broken glass.

Then Mercer did as he was told. "It was an Indian," he told the police, hating the way it sounded coming from his mouth. One of the cops, a black guy, just shook his head and went to find some other witnesses. The other officer, a hefty white guy with a goatee, leaned in a bit closer. "You know, technically the term's Native American. 'Indian' is seen as, uh, not exactly 'politically correct.'" He made air quotes with his fingers for every syllable of the final phrase, as if they were someone else's words.

Mercer nodded like he was hearing this for the first time.

"What can you do," the cop said, shrugging. "2016, you know? Can't say anything anymore."

8.

Mercer tried to convince the officers he was fine walking back to his dad's place, but they insisted he ride with them in the car. They assured him it was a favor, though the flashing lights made it feel like a punishment.

Evan, of course, was waiting at the screen door like a concerned mother. "What happened?"

It was a simple question; one Mercer knew belied the judgment just beneath the surface. "No trouble. Long story, but no—no trouble."

Evan's eyes were soft, like he thought Mercer was hiding something. Like he pitied him. "You want to talk?"

"I want to sleep."

"Merce. Come on. You just showed up in the back of a cop car at one in the morning. You're lucky you didn't wake Dad."

"Dad ate a handful of edibles today. Believe me, nothing's waking him." Mercer sat down on the couch and took off his shoes. "I'll tell you everything tomorrow."

"You sure?" Evan crossed his arms and arched his shoulders as high as his ears, as if the uncertainty of his brother's wellbeing had tensed every muscle in his body. All of it might've been comforting if it wasn't so hypocritical. This was Evan Moore, right? The Evan Moore who'd been kicked out of college for drunkenly pissing in the washing machines of every frat on campus? The Evan Moore who'd stolen his mom's ATM card and spent over three grand on a hotel party in

Atlantic City the night before the SATs? The Evan Moore who'd shown up to his own mother's funeral in a ruffled and sweaty suit, smelling of Old Granddad and Marlboro Lights? The one who had to be escorted out of the service by his sister-in-law before vomiting in the garden by the statue of Mary?

That Evan Moore?

Mercer didn't want to be an asshole. He was genuinely asking. He was asking because it seemed like everyone else had forgotten.

9.

Mercer awoke to the sounds of whistling and applause from the backyard, as if his father's dream of an auditorium had materialized overnight. The applause then turned to acoustic strumming and Mercer realized what was happening.

Of course. He was surprised he hadn't recognized it sooner. It was the soundtrack to everything his dad had ever deemed a project, the official score to the most mundane moments of his childhood. It was Eric Clapton's *Unplugged.*

The memories shot back into Mercer's mind. There they were, digging out a garden in the backyard in March 1995. "Before You Accuse Me" was playing and Lake turned the volume so loud that Alan from next door filed a formal noise complaint.

There they were, cleaning out the garage in October 1999, listening to the sexless, plodding version of. "He turned it into a blues song," Mercer remembered his dad saying. Mercer also remembered not caring.

And there they were again, dressing the Christmas tree in November 2000, with "Tears in Heaven" crackling through the living room stereo.

"Isn't this song about his dead kid?" Evan asked.

"He fell out of a window," Lake said, wrapping the lights around the tree.

"Can we listen to some Christmas carols?" Mercer remembered his mom asking.

"Let's just let the song finish," his dad said. "Would that be all right?"

Mercer poured some of the coffee his dad had made hours earlier and sat at the small kitchen table. He grabbed an index card from his bag and decided to keep it simple.

A	M
To Do (7/3/2016) · don't antagonize Dad · stay off social media · stop thinking about it	

Outside, Lake was at the end of the yard, up against the woods, measuring something on the ground as he called out numbers. Evan was beside him, pencil and notepad in hand.

"Our sleeping beauty," Lake said when he saw Mercer. "Couch all right?"

"That room's hot as anything."

Evan glared at him, clearly disappointed. Mercer took another sip of coffee.

"Maybe we can pick up a fan before tonight. Hey, do me a favor and get your shoes on in the next ten or so. If we're proactive, we can have the deck settling by mid-afternoon."

Mercer looked at the plot of earth in front of them. The only work he'd completed was the digging of four small holes, one for each corner of the deck. Puny yellow flags had been placed in each one, a detail his father had probably insisted on just to appear more professional. "When's the lumber arriving?"

"Any minute."

Mercer checked his watch. "Didn't you say they'd be here by 8?"

"Called him a bunch but got a voicemail every time. Probably on his way. Cell service cuts out on these roads all the time."

"Maybe he's just not coming."

"Guys in the trades always run late. That's just how it goes. Now get some shoes on. I wanna start the second he gets here."

Lake got back to distracting himself, measuring and re-measuring the distance between the holes. He laid out all of the tools they might need on the grass, triple-checking the drill bits and the charge on his nail gun. After an hour, there was still no wood.

When they were out of earshot, Mercer turned to Evan. "You think Dad paid this guy cash?"

"Hope not."

"I thought the deck was a bad idea. Maybe the lumber dude did, too."

"We might need to distract him. Delicately."

"There's a breakfast spot just a ways up the road."

Evan turned to him with genuine concern. "Is that where

you were last night?"

"Nearby."

"So, what happened? Did you get a citation or something?"

"It's a long story."

Evan motioned to their dad, who was counting out individual nails. "I've got time."

"I tried to get a beer, saw someone break a window. That's all. Cops gave me a lift."

Evan nodded, but Mercer knew he didn't buy the story. He'd told too many like it himself. "Don't go wandering like that."

"Couldn't sleep. Just needed to get out."

"We're in the sticks. Shit is different out here." Mercer couldn't remember the last time he'd heard his brother curse. Since he'd started dating Colleen, his few remaining rough edges had been sanded down. He'd begun smiling instead of disagreeing. He'd started using the word "delightful" without irony.

"Wake me up next time. I'll go with you," Evan said, still staring at their father. In the past few years, Mercer had sometimes forgotten Evan was the older brother. But there were those rare moments, despite all of the dumb shit Evan had done, despite years of behavior that disqualified him from acting as a protector, when Mercer still found himself comforted by gestures like that.

10.

They were half a dozen strong, their padded skin-tight suits advertising cycling clubs and races from previous weekends and distant towns. A few of them still wore the thick black shoes from their ride, clacking the ground as they walked by the Moore table and into the corner booth.

Mercer turned to his father, studying the leathered skin under his eyes. “You ever think about getting into cycling, Dad?”

Lake blew on his steaming coffee. “It’s expensive, isn’t it?”

“So’s weed.”

Lake laughed, blowing some of the coffee out of his mug and onto their table. As he cleaned it up with a handful of napkins, he kept chuckling. “Got me there,” he said, and Mercer knew that he’d snuck an edible before they’d hopped in the car.

“Have you ever thought about getting involved with any other hobbies now that you’re retired?” Evan asked.

“This isn’t another one of your little cards, is it? Is this an intervention? You have to tell me, right? Isn’t that part of it?”

Mercer studied the cyclists, trying to eavesdrop from a distance. They were unabashedly dorky, hollering about Major League Baseball and golf tournaments and their office jobs with the same intensity, still high on the endorphin rush from their early-morning ride. Despite their bloated stomachs and desperate attempts at hiding their male-pattern baldness,

Mercer couldn't deny that they looked happy.

His father had people in his life—neighbors, former co-workers, long-time clients, repeat grocery store clerks—but no one whom Mercer could confidently say was his friend. The only person who came close was someone who hadn't been around in years, an ex-hippie turned health-food wholesaler whose pastel clothes and long, greasy ponytail had always fascinated him and Evan when they were kids. The family called him Uncle Arthur, though Mercer's mom was always quick to remind him that Uncle Arthur wasn't actually family. "He's just one of your dad's friends," she'd say. "And he'll be leaving shortly."

As he studied his dad's glassy eyes and the way he laughed at the menu's seafood page, Mercer realized Arthur had probably just been his father's weed dealer.

11.

Lake didn't have any interests in high school; he had a job. The only music he listened to was what played on the jukeboxes at the Starview Diner, where he bussed tables. So, mostly Elton John and Olivia Newton-John. They seemed to be really into Johns over there.

There were Dead Heads at school, of course, but they seemed worlds away. He knew they smoked weed and that almost all of them had doctors for fathers. He knew they all wound up at Ivy League schools even though none of them seemed particularly bright. But that was about all he knew. To him, the band wasn't much more than that—a hobby for over-privileged kids who could afford to have hobbies.

It was four years later when a friend gave him a copy of *Europe 72*. He thought the songs were boring, but it made for decent background music while he worked on the Magnolia house, the one right behind the Jiffy Lube, he'd bought a year earlier. He'd be on the roof cleaning out the gutters or in the front yard rehabbing the walkway with "China Cat Sunflower" blaring from inside the house. All of the neighbors started calling him a hippy and he'd just laugh like he always did whenever someone said something he didn't understand.

That fall he took an Eastern Religions class at Glassboro State with a professor who pushed his long hair behind his ears. "There are many different paths to the same god," the guy said on the first day of class, and Lake spent the rest of the afternoon wandering through his other classes, turning the sentence over and over again in his mind.

The diner cut staff the next summer, so he found a job bar backing at the country club in Tavistock, the golf course that pretended it was a small town. That was where he met Arthur, the club's bartender, who wore a tie-dye shirt under the club's mandatory service uniform. He spoke with a manic intensity and told Lake that anyone who really knew him called him "the University of Arthur."

Lake felt like he was being tested. "Is that a joke?"

"Is it?" Arthur asked.

Lake didn't know how to respond, so he laughed. Arthur didn't blink. Lake tried again. "So, are you in school?"

He smiled. "I *am* school."

Sometimes it seemed like Arthur knew everything. At least once a shift, he was shocked by Lake's relative ignorance.

"How have you never listened to Canned Heat?"

"You don't know about Jonestown?"

"You never heard about Nixon's prosthetic dick?"

The questions weren't looking for answers: they were brief introductions to lengthy dissertations, always uttered with absolute certainty. After a while, Lake was tired of feeling stupid. He went to the empty library at Glassboro State and finally put his card to use, dedicating one night every week to studying everything Arthur had mentioned, everything he'd apparently missed in school.

He was surprised to find that Arthur's explanations were

often overstated. Sometimes they were flat-out wrong. Still, he thought, the library's dusty books weren't half as interesting as Arthur's version of the world.

They spent every shift break sneaking joints at the 18th hole, where Arthur would go on about the Dead. Sure, *Europe 72* was great, but how had he never heard *American Beauty?* Hadn't everyone heard *American Beauty?*

Sometimes, though, Arthur didn't want to talk about music, politics, or cults. "You ever think we're complicit?" he asked Lake one night.

"Working here?"

Arthur passed the joint back to Lake and then swung an imaginary putter towards the green. Lake had never smoked before that summer, not even a cigarette, but the breaks with Arthur made work so much easier. In fact, it was the first time he'd ever enjoyed working. As he moved from table to table, collecting empty wine glasses and discarded beer bottles, dodging overdone housewives and gin-blossomed insurance salesmen, he couldn't help but smile at the absurdity of the whole enterprise, couldn't help but find all of these people so unbelievably hilarious.

"It's the machinery in there," Arthur said, tossing the putter onto the ground. "And we're making them more comfortable!"

"I guess," Lake said, staring out into the navy-blue night. "We do make good tips, though."

12.

For Brigid O'Connor, there were numbers before words. On the day she was born, her mother spent hours repeating the word "ma-ma" to her, emphasizing each syllable and drawing out the "m" to try and make it stick. It was a routine she'd repeat every day for the next eight months, but her baby girl was still babbling nonsense. So, she gave up on names and instead started counting. Suddenly, Brigid wouldn't shut up.

In grade school, Brigid recited her multiplication tables every night at dinner. During dessert, she'd ask her dad to try stumping her with triple-digit problems. After he tossed one at her, she'd close her eyes to see the equation, carrying the numbers in the air with her pointer finger. When she'd found the answer, her eyes would pop open, and she'd scream the number. Her father would type the problem into a calculator to check the answer, smiling when he proved her right. It happened every time.

Sacred Heart High School for Girls didn't offer calculus until Brigid demanded it for her junior year. A month into the course, she decided it hadn't been worth the trouble—the man assigned to teach it, a painfully shy waif who'd only finished undergraduate the year before, was clearly over his head. He'd often screw up proofs on the board, relying almost entirely on Brigid's input to correct his mistakes. At the end of the year, she received an A-, despite nearly flawless tests. "Class participation was often dismissive and disruptive," he'd written.

It was the same in every class. Brigid was told she was too loud or disrespectful when she calmly pointed out the obvious. In her senior year theology class, they learned the Rhythm Method, tracing their cycles on branded Sacred Heart calendars. The teacher was Sister Mary Ellen, a 20-year-old who earnestly spoke about the joys of her celibacy. The school had assigned Sister Mary Ellen to the class because they thought the girls would admire her, and many of them did, even if on the weekends they'd still park with their boyfriends and ignore her advice about waiting until marriage.

Brigid wasn't one of those girls. She didn't have a boyfriend, for one, and she thought Mary Ellen was a fool. "Aren't you angry you can't be a priest?" she asked her one class. A few of the other girls murmured in disbelief, confirming for Brigid that she was on to something.

"I was called to serve God in my current role, Ms. O'Connor."

"But aren't you angry you can't serve God like a man?"

Sister Mary Ellen tried to smile. She'd spent the previous night preparing a detailed lesson on tithes and could sense it slipping through her delicate fingers. "I've just told you—I don't want to be a priest. It's of no interest to me. Being a nun is my *vocation.* I was called—"

"But doesn't it anger you that a man has dictated what you can or cannot be?"

"You're angry because someone has told you 'no.'" Sister pointed her index finger at Brigid, accusing her. "That's what this really comes down to, isn't it?"

Brigid smiled. "It is, Mary. I'm angry that an old, sexless man has told me 'no.'" She paused to study the horror on the young nun's face, knowing it would be the only thing that would make the trip to the principal's office worthwhile.

She assumed college would be different. She assumed that there were parts of the world that would finally understand what she'd been trying to say for all those years. She wanted things to change, and they did, but it was hard to say if they improved.

She went to Rutgers because it was affordable. Her gen ed requirements were impersonal lectures where her professors read from books they'd published years earlier. Her academic advisor encouraged her to take Business Math rather than the real thing, suggesting she'd never find a career if she didn't get more practical. The only person she talked to was her roommate Debbie, a princess from Bergen County, who didn't seem to understand how someone could be so disappointed with the college experience. Her only advice was to rush a sorority.

By the time exams came around, Brigid knew she'd be dropping out. Not that she told anyone. Part of her wanted to tell her mother, to finally have an honest conversation with her, but she couldn't find the words. Every time she practiced a speech in her head, she imagined her mother's response. It was always the same: why do you think you've got it so bad?

She skipped the conversation and hopped a bus to Long Beach Island, where her uncle owned a diner, arriving unannounced just a few hours after her final exam. Her uncle didn't technically have any openings, but he could add a night shift if she didn't complain about the shitty tips.

"Does your mother know you're here?" he asked. He was aware that his sister wasn't the easiest woman in the world, but he didn't want to be accused of disloyalty.

"She will," Brigid said.

"Then I'm guessing you need a place to stay," he said. "You know we've got an extra room at the house." He hadn't said it, but she knew the arrangement wouldn't truly be free. She'd be expected to babysit his kids, her cousins, a few nights a week. Any time she'd seen her aunt try to discipline them they'd only grown more unruly. They were tiny nightmares, incorrigible, ungrateful runts.

"I've actually got a place," she said. It was a lie.

An hour later she signed a contract for a seasonal room at the L.B.I. Motel, a spot notorious on the island. It was a flophouse, filled with rail-thin addicts and underage kids looking for a place to party. Still, it was better than babysitting her cousins. At least the prostitutes offered cigarettes.

And even though the sheets smelled liked dry-cleaned piss and every morning brought another needle to her doorstep, it felt good to pay the weekly rent out of her own pocket, to feel like she was an adult for the first time in her life.

The plan was to make enough money to make it to the west coast in the fall. There were no specifics beyond that. She knew that meant it was far from an actual plan. She hated the uncertainty of it, but she was determined to let it remain vague.

The uncertainty was the point. She'd spent every year of her life plotting and planning, only to find herself depressed and alone in New Brunswick.

Embrace the question mark, she told herself. Stop doing so much. See what happens when you allow life to string you along. Whenever she dealt with a particularly obnoxious table at the diner or listened to another 3 a.m. fight in the Motel parking lot, she imagined herself off on a bus, headed towards some unknowable destination.

13.

Lake and Arthur made the drive to L.B.I. every Saturday after the late shift, splitting a six pack on the drive. As he drove, Arthur would go on about the wives from the club that he was going to bang—about how they must hate their accountant husbands, how they'd trapped themselves in loveless marriages, how suburbia was a well-hidden prison. Lake half-listened and stared out the open window, admiring the way the Pines along Route 72 seemed to go on forever.

On the island, they'd stay at a house everyone called The Police Station. Sunlight, Arthur's friend whose legal name was on the lease, was a summer cop on the island. It was an odd job for someone who'd spent the previous summer growing his hair and selling nitrous balloons at J.F.K. Stadium, but the Surf City PD still gave him a badge, a gun, and a squad car. He hadn't done anything to earn all that except agree to work for minimum wage.

Arthur said Sunlight could afford the house's rent because he had a trust fund. Arthur said that Sunlight was so wealthy that his family traced its heritage back to the Mayflower. Arthur said that Sunlight's family had made millions from war profiteering, though when Lake asked for specifics he was dodgy, claiming that he couldn't say too much. "You start talking about that and you end up with a target on your head," he said. Lake wanted to ask him why they continued sleeping there if the house was the product of blood money. He never did, though, because he really liked having a reliable place to crash at the shore.

Even if privilege was something Sunlight already knew well, he relished the prestige that came with being an officer on the force. He used the badge to get free coffee at the corner store and the gun to impress girls who didn't know any better. The car was the real perk, though. No matter how loud their parties got or how many people they squeezed on the deck, the sight of the squad car in front of the house was enough to deter the neighbors from calling in a complaint.

Sunlight loved what the job provided him, but was troubled by the fact that he'd become The Man. It was especially bad whenever Arthur convinced him they should take a bong rip. "I'm really a pacifist," he'd say, staring at his badge. "I'm a peacemaker."

Brigid had been on the island for two weeks before she finally wound up at The Police Station. Another girl from the restaurant had suggested they swing by before going out to the bars. "It's a bunch of stoners," she'd said. "But they usually have a keg."

That night, Brigid had planned on heading back to the Motel and calling her mom, figuring she finally owed her an honest conversation. But there was an offer right there in front of her, one that sounded like the college experience she hadn't had. She had told herself that she needed to be more spontaneous, and she wanted to make good on that resolution, even if the thought of being more spontaneous made her stomachache.

Years and years later, when Lake and Brigid talked about that night with their boys, they told them it was a friend's BBQ in the middle of the afternoon. They did not mention that their first conversation came after they'd both taken pulls from Sunlight's bong, or that it sent them into crippling coughing fits. They did not mention that their first kiss was actually a sloppy, handsy affair on Sunlight's stained thrift store couch or that the rest of the party had cheered them on.

Lake didn't consider the sanitized version of the story a lie. It wasn't factual, but it wasn't untrue. In his eyes, the most important part of the story was the feeling he had when he first saw Brigid enter The Police Station. "I knew I was going to be with her," he'd say every year on their anniversary, when he'd force the boys to sit through the whole elaborate myth. "I felt like we'd been reunited after a lifetime apart."

After Brigid passed, Lake stopped telling that story. It was too depressing to think about how much had changed since then. It was even more depressing to realize how few specifics he remembered—there was Brigid's face when she entered the room, the color of the couch, and the way she detailed her plans to finally escape New Jersey, but everything else had faded into the dusty recesses of his mind. Almost all of his memories had become recollections of decontextualized feelings. What he knew was he had felt whole that night. That was about it.

So much happened in the years to follow, even if Lake couldn't remember the specifics. Maybe that's obvious.

Everything happened after that night.

A year after that night, he and Brigid were engaged. They held a traditional family wedding in New Jersey before leaving that life behind them. Lake bought a pickup with a camper cabin so they could make their way out west. Arthur had friends in Washington who would let them crash for a few weeks. They knew they could figure it out from there.

Two years after that night, they began the drive back to New Jersey. Arthur hadn't mentioned that his friends in Washington were living in a roach-infested commune. They spent their days selling barely edible health food products and their nights lavishing praise on the owner of the house, an obnoxious Bard dropout who spoke about vibrations and healing crystals. Lake and Brigid bailed after a few days, then spent a few weeks at campgrounds in Oregon, wandering around the state's tiny hamlets in search of paying jobs. They picked apples at an organic farm outside Eugene and clipped weed for some back-to-the-land types near Corvallis. After a few months, they finally admitted they were exhausted.

Five years after that night, Arthur was busted trying to sell cocaine to an undercover cop. He pleaded guilty and did a few years, which he said, "weren't as bad as you'd think." Eight years after that night, he married a woman he'd met at a blackjack table in Reno. Twelve years after that night, he paid his old friend Lake an unannounced visit in National Park after years of silence. He had gifts for the kids, but Brigid kept Evan and Mercer upstairs. "You let a convicted criminal into our house," Brigid said afterward, her voice low so the boys wouldn't hear from the other room.

Seven years after that night, Brigid said she wanted a job, even if it was part-time or mindless or even demeaning—she just wanted to feel like she was contributing. She wanted to sign deposit slips and complain about her boss like anyone else. Lake did the math: daycare was more expensive than Brigid staying at home. And wasn't it better that they're spending these years at home rather than in some dirty playroom? Wasn't it better that it's one of their parents rather than some stranger? Brigid always said yes. Of course, she did. "It just makes sense when you add it all up," she told the neighbors. But the truth was that most days she didn't know. Most days things weren't as simple as the numbers made them seem.

Eleven years after that night, Brigid and Lake began couples counseling. Brigid appreciated finally having a mediator. It was nice to know that what she was saying made sense when she heard it out loud. She talked about her frustrations with the boys, about her isolation on those endless weekdays, about the fact that they'd stopped having sex. Lake nodded along through every meeting, but his agitation showed in subtle ways. "This woman's making a killing off of us," he said every time he signed the therapist's checks.

Twenty-five years after that night, Sunlight left rehab and went swimming in the brown water of the Pine Barrens. He'd later claim that it was the swim and not the program that healed him. He bought a few hundred acres in the Pines with the inheritance from some dead relative and began what he referred to on his cryptic website as Cultural Philanthropy.

Thirty-four years after that night, Brigid died in the living room of their house in National Park. The last person she spoke to was a friend from high school. Brigid told her that Alejandra, her daughter-in-law, had never thanked her for the Christmas gifts. “Is that a generational thing?” she’d asked her friend. “I can’t believe I’m saying, ‘kids these days’ but I think I’m saying, ‘kids these days.’”

Thirty-six years after that night, Lake was at a cabin in the woods, leaving angry messages on the voicemail of a contractor after a hearty breakfast. His sons stood nearby, trying to think of some way to calm him down.

14.

Evan insisted they get away from the cabin for the day and forget about the deck. Father Brad had encouraged him to plan some fallback activities for the weekend in the event that spending time together itself didn't feel productive. "Always have a backup plan," he'd told him. "Always have the next step."

For a family that'd never been interested in hunting or fishing, the options in the Pines were limited. The shore was only another 40 minutes east, but he knew his father would complain about the holiday crowds. There was antiquing nearby, but if he even suggested that as a possibility his brother would never let him live it down.

So, it would have to be hiking, and even that drew some complaints. "Walking," his dad said, correcting him. "I've never understood why people think it's anything more than that."

Evan decided he'd play tour guide—even if they were unhappy, he'd narrate his way through it, maybe even take their minds off themselves for a few hours. As he drove, he explained they were headed to the Batona Trail, which wound 50 miles from Little Egg Harbor through Wharton State Forest and up to Ong's Hat, spanning all of the Pines. Lake feigned interest from the passenger seat while Mercer read headlines in the back. Elie Wiesel had died, Trump swore he wasn't anti-Semitic, and the Phillies had been crushed by the Royals. He took out his index card and grabbed a pen from the center console.

A	M
TO DO (7/3/2016) · don't antagonize Dad · stay off social media · stop thinking about it	COLLECTED "Trump has also previously retweeted tweets from apparent neo-Nazi supporters, including one from the account @WhiteGenocideTM, which also tweeted numerous quotes from Nazi propagandist Joseph Goebbels." When did Evan become a nature enthusiast?

As his brother went on about the unique ecology of the Pines, Mercer stared at his to-do list. He doubted Alejandra would be posting anything, wherever she was, but he was still curious. Maybe there were clues in her likes. Maybe she was regretting the letter.

He returned to his phone and found a message from a number he didn't recognize. His stomach clenched: it had to be Alejandra. She'd needed a break (understandable) and a new phone to make that happen (plausible), but now she was ready to return.

He was disappointed when he actually read the message.

please remember to listen!! praying 4 u

"Did you add me to some Catholic listserv?" he asked his brother, who was genuinely confused at the question. Mercer read the text out loud to prove he wasn't losing his mind.

"Spam," his dad said. "I get shit like that all the time. Delete and move on."

Mercer stared at the screen for a minute before replying.

Wrong number.

no sir

UNSUBSCRIBE.

not a bot

Okay, then who is this?

not important

Evan parked the car and told them they'd need to walk a little to the trail head. Mercer placed the phone under the seat, where it continued buzzing.

just remember to listen

then things will becme clearer

become*

15.

The Emilio Carranza Memorial is located on Route 206, just a quarter mile after the gravel road turns into sand. It's a big, heaping stone monument, something between an obelisk and an Aztec ruin. No matter the time of year, it's surrounded by bouquets and hand-written notes. In the middle of the desolate Pines, its existence feels like a mistake.

Evan explained what he'd read about Carranza to his dad and brother. In 1928, everyone in America was talking about Lindbergh's transatlantic flight. After he flew to Mexico City, a few Mexican politicians were so wrapped up in the spectacle they decided they needed their own Lindbergh. Emilio Carranza, a military hero at the age of 18 and the country's most famous aviator by 22, was the obvious choice.

Evan pulled up a portrait and showed them his phone. After a bad crash in Sonora, Carranza had the bones in his face set with platinum screws, making it look like he was hiding chaw in his cheeks. But Mercer couldn't believe how childish he looked: his aviator's jacket was two sizes too big, as if he'd stolen it from his father's closet.

The politicians built a replica of Lindbergh's *Spirit of St. Louis* plane and called it *The Mexico-Excelsior*. They wanted Carranza to fly from Mexico City to New York City and then back again—it was a stunt that only Lindbergh himself would dare to attempt. Carranza made it to New York without a problem, but the return trip was marred by complications. There was bad weather, and he was forced to delay the flight for three days. After all, *The Mexico-Excelsior* was a tiny plane. It was a wise decision, the politicians said. It showed Carranza was not only brave but smart.

Then on the fourth day, as the storm continued raging, Carranza suddenly took off.

Why? Why not wait one more day? It was all because some asshole sent him a telegram. "Leave immediately," the asshole said, "or the quality of your manhood will be in doubt." Never doubt the power of a faceless taunt.

The Mexico-Excelsior couldn't handle the storm. Carranza's body was eventually found in the Pines by a couple of blueberry pickers who described the horror of finding a flashlight lodged through the young man's hand. The autopsy determined that, in his final moments, he'd been trying to find a safe place to crash. The telegram was still in his breast pocket.

Evan lectured on as Mercer studied the memorial. Schoolchildren in Mexico had raised money for the monument with penny drives, sending the lump sum to the American Legion so their hero would be remembered forever. At the base of the monument, it read: THE PEOPLE OF MEXICO HOPE THAT YOUR HIGH IDEALS WILL BE REALIZED.

Mercer didn't know what they were talking about. He didn't know that Carranza had had any high ideals, at least not what Evan said. All he could see was the skinny kid in the long aviator's jacket, scanning the tops of the Pines with his flashlight, knowing it was no one's fault but his own.

16.

Evan led Lake and Mercer into the woods, pointing to the pink blazes on the trees that would let them know if they'd lost their way.

"Feel that under your feet?" Evan asked. "See how white the ground is? Locals call it sugar sand."

On both sides of the trail were towering walls of pitch pine. Mercer studied the thin trees, amazed at how they swayed in unison with the wind. It made him feel like they were walking through the hallway of a hazy dream.

Lake turned around to Mercer and held up his palms, silently instructing him to slow down. Evan kept walking and talking, leaving Mercer and his dad out-of-earshot.

"I'm going to eat another gummy," Lake said in a whisper. "You interested?"

He guessed this was his dad's way of apologizing for the argument from the night before. Mercer held out his hand, happy to receive his father's penance.

Twenty minutes later, Evan was explaining how ten thousand years earlier the Leni Lenape had inhabited the land, long before the Swedish and the Dutch or the British; how hundreds of millions of years before *that* the Atlantic coastal plain began to form; how thousands upon thousands of minerals were deposited into the ground they were standing on; how cedar, oak, and pine trees began to grow there after the last ice age. Mercer and his father listened in silence, awed at the millions of years of history they'd stumbled upon.

"Beneath the Pinelands lies a huge natural reservoir of pure water, estimated at 17 trillion gallons," Evan read from the trail guide. "That's enough to cover all of New Jersey in ten feet of water."

Mercer repeated the number out loud, dumbfounded. His steps grew a little lighter, an unintended consequence of learning what lay beneath them. He turned to his father, who flashed a wide grin.

"Hey, Merce," he said. "We're *walking* on *water*."

17.

As they drove away from the trail, they studied the hand-painted roadside signs along the Pines' winding sand roads. There were plenty for blueberries and tomatoes, pointing toward unmanned wooden stands. There was one for the BED AND BISCUIT BNB, which featured cartoon dogs sleeping in nightcaps and pajamas. There was one for DON'S SPORTS CENTER, which advertised itself as a one-stop athletic authority, though when they drove by the actual building Mercer noticed it was just an abandoned garage.

"You think anyone's selling fireworks?" Lake asked.

"They're illegal in New Jersey," Evan said. "Plus, the townships all have official displays. Just like in National Park."

"No, I know. But I wanted to shoot some off from the cabin. Christen the new place."

"Should've told me before I left the city," Mercer said. "I could've filled the trunk."

Evan saw an opportunity. "We can find something tonight. A lot of townships do the 3rd, just like in National Park. I'll take a look if you want."

"I just had this image of the sky in the backyard all lit up."

"There must be some enterprising young Piney selling explosives," Mercer said. He'd intended it as a joke, then realized it was probably true. There were signs every quarter mile or so advertising corn and eggs and firewood and hubcaps. Was it really that hard to imagine fireworks?

They drove aimlessly for a while, ostensibly in search of illegal explosives but mostly just trying to kill some time. It was Lake who finally suggested they follow the one that read: BLUEGRASS & BBQ — CELEBRATE AMERICA **TODAY**!

"They might not have fireworks," he said, "but I am starving."

When they arrived, there were too many shirts to count.

TRUMP 2016: DRAIN THE SWAMP

TRUMP: REAL AMERICAN HERO

HILLARY FOR PRISON

TRUMP THAT BITCH

A pale woman stood in line for the pies, smiling as she waved a miniature flag of Trump's face. In big, block letters it read: FUCK YOUR FEELINGS.

Mercer had expected the shirts. He'd read enough profiles of places like the Pines, where industry had left, and heroin was killing those who'd stayed behind. He'd read that a lot of the people out there thought all politicians were full of shit; Trump, by admitting that he was full of shit, was respectable. He didn't understand any of it, really, but he'd read it all.

But flags were new for Mercer. He couldn't recall any other presidential candidate who'd inspired that level of devotion. You pledged allegiance to a flag. People died for flags. Mercer tried to recall seeing a Hillary flag in the city, but the closest thing he could remember was seeing an I'M WITH HER tote bag at brunch.

They grabbed Chinet plates and packed them high with ribs, burgers, slaw, potato salad, and huckleberry pie. The band at the gazebo started up into "Midnight Flyer" and Lake whistled along, even though he didn't know the melody. "This is good for us, y'know?" he said. "Spend some time out of the bubble."

The articles Mercer had read on The Trump Appeal all suggested that metropolitan liberals were ignorant of the plight of the rural, white, working class. Most of them suggested their liberal readers strike up conversations with Trump voters. We should all be informed, they argued: we should understand what the Democrats are doing wrong.

Mercer had never attempted that conversation. And as he eyed a man at the picnic table across from them who'd draped a Confederate flag from the back of his electric wheelchair, he decided he would keep it that way.

18.

Ethan Music Hall

From Wikipedia, the free encyclopedia

The **Ethan Music Hall** is a concert hall located in the Pinelands of New Jersey. The hall traces its history back to the Ethan Brothers, who are credited with playing an integral part in the development of northeastern American bluegrass and folk music. [1]

History [edit]

1900s [edit]

The Ethan brothers built a shack deep in the woods at the turn of the 20th century so they'd have a place to play their music, which they simply referred to as "the songs." At first it was just the two of them. Edwin was on an acoustic guitar that was always slipping out-of-tune. His younger brother Michael played a homemade fiddle. "The songs" were what they'd grown up with, which were mostly religious hymns their grandfather had sung at family gatherings. Sometimes they also set music to folk tales they'd overheard at the general store in Tabernacle.[2]

New Jersey bluegrass group The Piney Pickers memorialized the brothers in their song "Edwin and Michael." [3] According to the song, Edwin would occasionally attempt to sing, but he was shaky and uncertain, so he delivered the lyrics in a wooden monotone, like he was "recitin' a poem at the direction of his teacher." After a few weeks of playing "the songs," the Ethan Brothers invited some friends to join them at the shack. They brought instruments, and voices, and whiskey. Edwin cooked some pork salt over a fire and smiled, happy to host and even happier to have someone else sing. [4] [*page needed*]

Word spread. People came from Bass River and Tuckerton. One family traveled three hours from Salem because someone had told them it was the best music he'd ever heard. "The songs" were no longer defined by the Ethan brothers, though the two of them were surprised by how similar the others' songs sounded to their own. Even if Edwin had never heard a visitor's song before, all he needed was the first few notes and he knew where it was headed from there.[5]

2000s [edit]

The original shack was condemned in 1999, but a fundraiser led to the construction of the Ethan Music Hall in 2002.[6] In the present day, the hall fosters the same communal spirit that the brothers had found so inspiring so many years earlier. [*citation needed*]

Evan looked up from reading the page aloud. Neither of them had been listening: his brother was lost in his thoughts, staring at the picnic table across from them, while his father had closed his eyes, nodding along with the band on stage.

The website made the relationship sound so easy, as if families naturally worked together to create something bigger than themselves. He didn't know what he expected from a Wikipedia article. Anyone could've written that entry, he thought, even if they had no idea what they were talking about.

19.

Colleen called at 5:30, just like she did every day. "I know I said I wouldn't bug you, but I just got out of Mass and wanted to check in. I'm sorry!"

When Evan told her that he was standing in the parking lot, listening to out-of-key bluegrass, she said it sounded like fun. A pickup with Trump flags rolled into the parking lot. "Plenty of characters," he said. "That's for sure."

"How're things with Mercer?"

"Hard to say. At any given moment he's either looking at his phone or picking fights with Dad."

"Well, hey." He could hear her trying to find an upbeat spin. "Did you try the Conversation Starters?"

"Unmitigated disaster. Mercer was disgusted. Dad was insulted."

"Everything takes time," she said. "I believe in you, Evan Moore." This was a rhetorical trick of hers, using his full name like he was some great historical figure rather than a schlubby guy in his thirties who lived with his dad. "Remember: the Vatican wasn't built in a day," she said. "That was in Father Brad's homily tonight. I *immediately* thought of you."

It was objectively corny. It was such a dumb saying that suggested even the most boilerplate clichés weren't quite enough for Catholics. Evan knew it was idiotic, something intended for someone three times his age and with far more religious conviction. And yet, he couldn't help feeling moved.

Maybe it was Colleen's enthusiasm, or maybe it was the absolute sincerity with which she'd relayed it, but he had to laugh—at the fact that he loved this woman, that he was at an impromptu Trump rally in the Pines, that he of all people was attempting to bring what remained of his family together.

Colleen chuckled along cautiously, worried she'd done something wrong. "What's so funny?"

"Ah, I don't know." Evan turned from the parking lot to find his brother and father, who were watching the Piney Pickers start a song about the birth of the Jersey Devil. "Everything, I guess."

20.

At first, Mercer assumed he was mistaken. A part of him wondered if his dad's gummy had sat with him longer than he'd anticipated—this had to be a soft-hallucination, a bit of his subconscious peeking its head out into reality. There was no way that Nan, the flip-flopped, brick-throwing kid from the night before was actually at the cookout selling Trump gear.

He would've walked away if Nan hadn't called out to him, eagerly pushing his M.A.G.A.-filled shopping cart in Mercer's direction. "How did things end up last night?"

"I think you should keep your voice down."

"Ah, fuck that. We're good here. Did they stop you? Did you tell them it was an Indian?"

An elderly woman with a walker approached the shopping cart and asked if she could have an XXL hoodie. "For my grandson," she said with a smile. Nan handed her the sweatshirt and thanked her for her patriotism.

"These are free?"

"You don't want one, right? I mean, you can have one, but I didn't take you for a Trump guy." He squinted, evaluating Mercer. "Maybe Jill Stein?"

"You shouldn't be out in public. The cops are looking for you. The guys at the bar said they had video."

"I appreciate the concern, but I'm fine. I'm working."

"You're giving out free clothes."

"That's a good way of looking at it. I like that. Makes me

feel better about everything: I'm not handing out Trump merch, I'm giving out free clothes. It's nice to feel good about it. You know what I mean?"

"That woman didn't pay you."

"Right. She didn't have to. I work for a guy. That guy pays me to do things. This afternoon it's handing out Trump shit at a redneck BBQ. This morning it was driving to PA and buying five grand worth of fireworks. And tomorrow? Well, actually, I have tomorrow off."

21.

When Father Brad told Evan to head to the Pines with Mercer and Lake, he framed it as an opportunity for Evan to work on one of the goals he'd written down months earlier: *I want to re-build the relationship with my brother.*

Father Brad grabbed a legal pad and a pen and handed them to Evan. He wanted him to write a letter to his brother and name all of the things he'd been wanting to get off of his chest. "Be as specific as you'd like, but don't deal in metaphors. Be literal. Be direct. Say exactly how you feel."

Evan didn't know where to begin. He wondered if that was part of the exercise—that Brad would watch him struggle for ten minutes and then tell him this was an object lesson about the myth of easy solutions. But when he saw him staring at the blank yellow page, Brad asked for the pad and quickly scribbled something.

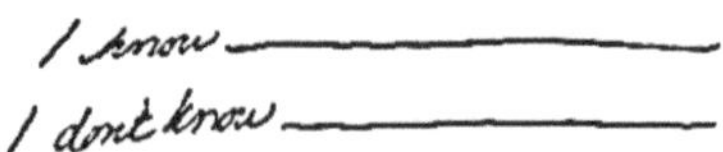

"Fill in the blanks," Father Brad said. Evan was done in ten seconds.

I know YOU DON'T LIKE ME ANYMORE
I don't know WHY WE DON'T TALK ABOUT MOM

"Now we're getting somewhere," Father Brad said.

22.

The boys dropped Lake at home and said they were running to the store for beer and seltzer. They were giddy when their father bought the lie without question, laughing as they pulled out of his driveway, imagining how shocked he'd be when they returned with a trunk full of Nan's free fireworks.

"He might actually shit himself," Mercer said. "Or he'll be passed out before we even make it back."

Evan removed an index card from his pocket, placing it on his thigh. He re-read all the statements he and Brad had written at the last session, trying to find the perfect one to lead with.

Mercer noticed it from the corner of his eye. "Is that my to-do list?"

"No," Evan said, and turned it over on his lap. "You're still doing those?"

"Sometimes," he lied. "It's a good way to organize everything."

"Did you do one for today?"

Mercer nodded. "Told myself I wouldn't antagonize Dad. Been successful there. Also told myself I wouldn't think about Alejandra. Resounding defeat on that one."

"Well, we can't control our thoughts."

Mercer remembered who he was talking with. "Right."

Evan turned the card over again and eyed the statements. He wanted to begin with one that felt natural, so Mercer would be more willing to engage. "If he's not," Brad had said, "he'll try and derail the whole exercise."

"Do you actually believe that?" Mercer said.

Evan was caught off-guard. "Believe what?"

"About controlling our thoughts. I mean, I know you're probably working on that in therapy, but isn't your time in AA really just a long process of trying to think about something other than drinking?"

Evan nodded, waiting a full ten seconds before responding, just like he and Brad had practiced. "I hear you," he said. "But the way we think and the thoughts we have aren't the same."

"Semantics."

"I'm serious."

"Bet you are."

"Take last night."

"Taking it."

"When you and dad were drinking, I thought it would be nice to have a beer with them. But then I forced myself to think about what having that beer would mean. What it might lead to. And that's what made me feel okay about not drinking, even though I had that thought."

Mercer was quiet for a beat. His brother was right, but he didn't want to say that out loud. "How much does Colleen know about the old you?"

"I gave her the cliff notes. Vomiting, fighting, trouble, shame. I didn't include the pissy sheets."

Mercer laughed. "You were also pissing people for a while there. What was your freshman year roommate's name?"

"Ricky," Evan said. "Jesus."

"That poor guy." They sat in silence for a few seconds, unsure of where to go next. "Do you want to put some music on?"

"Why're you asking about Colleen?"

Mercer shrugged, his eyes still on the road. "Seems pretty serious between you two. Didn't know if there was a point when you gave her the unabridged version."

Evan hadn't considered it before. "You think I should?"

"I don't know if I'm the one who should be giving out relationship advice." Mercer forced a laugh and looked in the rearview mirror, though there was no one else on the road. "So, what's with the index card?"

Evan had forgotten about the statements on his lap. "It was an exercise I did with Brad."

"The priest."

He could sense the judgment in his brother's voice but decided to ignore it. "We've been talking about being more direct. So, we did an exercise. Like, a practice run, I guess. He had me create a list of direct statements that I wanted to put out there."

"'Put out there,' like, to the world?"

"Like, to you."

"Oh," Mercer said. "All right."

"Do you want me to read them?"

"I don't know. Do you want to?"

"It's supposed to be good exercise."

"All right. But do you want to do it?"

"I think it's a way to try and cut through what we're doing right now."

"What're we doing right now?"

"Trying to avoid talking."

There was another beat. "Okay."

Evan looked down at the index card and took a deep breath.

I KNOW YOU'RE SCARED ABOUT THE FUTURE.
I DON'T KNOW WHY YOU CAN'T TALK TO ME ABOUT IT.

I KNOW YOU'RE UPSET WITH YOURSELF.
I DON'T KNOW WHY YOU FEEL LIKE YOU CAN'T CHANGE.

I KNOW YOU DON'T LIKE ME ANYMORE.
I DON'T KNOW WHY WE DON'T TALK ABOUT MOM.

Mercer turned onto a white sand road, causing a cloud of dust to surround the car. Evan had stared intently at the index card while reading his statements, but now he turned to his brother to gauge his reaction.

"I don't dislike you, Ev," Mercer said, staring out the windshield. His voice was wavering, so he paused to steady himself. "I just don't know what to say most of the time. I don't even know where to start."

Evan patted his brother's shoulder, squeezing the skin beside his neck. He wanted more answers, he wanted to know everything, but he didn't need them right then. He knew there would be time.

"Could you do me a favor?" Mercer asked.

"Sure thing."

"Could you put on some music?" Mercer grabbed his phone from the cup holder, wriggling out from under his brother's hand. "I think we could use some music."

23.

The road was lined with wilted houses whose porches swayed in the wind. Overgrown lawns were littered with windowless cars and mismatched plastic chairs. After several unmarked miles, the brothers found their destination. "You'll know it when you see," Nan had said. "There's nothing else like it." He was right. It was a single-story circle, an octagonal cupola whose design seemed to defy physics. In the middle of the Pines, it might as well have been a grounded UFO.

Nan was on the yellowed lawn, sitting next to an older man in a baggy white suit that'd been stained by years of backwoods living. Evan muttered something about turning around, but Mercer put the car in park and waved. "Say hello to the creepy people, Evan."

The brothers exited the car, and the older man began walking toward them. He'd lost the hair on top of his head but had let the rest grow into a long white ponytail. As he got closer, Mercer could hear water sloshing around in his knee-high rain boots. "Ben Faunce the Third," he said, eagerly shaking both of their hands. The brothers introduced themselves and Faunce furrowed his brow like he recognized them. "You're not from here."

"No," Mercer said. "Philly."

"We grew up in National Park," Evan corrected.

"The old oil refinery? The family used to do a lot of business there. Don't remember much of a town, but I was so young then. Your family—they worked on the refinery?"

"Our dad started his own business. Technology help."

"One of the first in the area," Evan added.

"Amazing," Faunce said. "Just amazing. The ingenuity of our people never ceases to astound me. We're capable of so much when we're unfettered. Don't you think so?"

Mercer looked around, trying to spot the promised fireworks. Nan was no help; he was studying his phone, bored with the entire exchange.

"I'd be so absolutely honored if you all would join me for a drink. Can I invite you inside?"

"My brother's sober," Mercer said, hoping that cutting the pleasantries might move things along.

Faunce laughed. "So am I!"

The inside of the roundhouse was as welcoming as a fallout shelter. Mercer looked for a bed, or a couch, or at least a sleeping bag, but found none. The octagon's walls were lined with unmarked cardboard boxes, each one a unique size and peculiar hue of brown. Mercer suddenly felt lightheaded. Even though he knew it was impossible, it felt like the circle was slowly closing in on him.

Nan pulled one of the boxes from the wall and delicately placed it on the ground. He took out a small cooler and removed two glass bottles.

"I hope you forgive the state of my home. It's always a mess around the holidays," Faunce said. "But it's worth it. I love what I do."

"And what do you do?" Evan asked.

"You've heard of Take A Pop? The soft drink?" He pointed to the unmarked boxes, as if it'd been obvious that they were filled with soda. "My grandfather was the inventor. Which makes me the heir to the throne, so to speak." He waited for a reaction, but the brothers only nodded. He smiled tightly, trying to hide his disappointment. Nan popped the caps from the bottles and handed them to Evan and Mercer.

It tasted like flat Pepsi, like what used to come out of the fountain at the Wawa when some overworked employee forgot to change out the expired syrup. It was hard to imagine this was the source of generational wealth. Mercer prayed he wouldn't be expected to drink more than one.

"My grandfather was a pharmacist. He invented this for sick kids—supposed to clear up your sinuses and ease tension in your chest. We've long said it keeps memory sharp, especially in older folks, though we've never run studies." His mind went elsewhere for a second and he took out a small notepad from his pocket. He quickly scribbled something down before returning his attention to Mercer and Evan. "On its face, it was a soft drink. A treat. But its enjoyment was just a byproduct. My grandfather cared deeply about his neighbors. He cared deeply about his countrymen. And I believe that led him to his invention."

"The soda," Evan said.

"The recipe," Faunce said. "Yes."

"And now you run the company?"

"Philosophically, yes. In a managerial sense? No, not technically. I leave the pencil pushing to some wonderful employees of mine. It allows me to carry on my grandfather's philanthropy. And I work at it every day, Evan, I really do. I moved here nearly twenty years ago. I was in a bad place—physically, spiritually, and emotionally. I'd tried to run from my family's legacy. And this was the place that saved me. I mean that quite literally. It was the land that saved me. Of course, Nan's people have known this since the dawn of time."

Mercer looked to Nan, who rolled his eyes.

"The water in this area of the world has been proven to rejuvenate human life. Twenty years running, and I still walk around with it in my boots." He kicked with his right foot and sloshed some of the pond water around.

Nan cleared his throat. "Think my shift's up."

Faunce apologized, took out his wallet, and handed him a stack of hundreds. As Nan walked away counting his money, Faunce nodded at the brothers. "Good kid," he said in a low voice.

"He's an employee?" Mercer asked.

"He's not on the Take A Pop payroll, no. But he works for me on what I consider my philanthropic outreach. Today, that meant buying as many fireworks from Pennsylvania as humanly possible."

"And the Trump shirts?" Mercer asked.

"Exactly!" Faunce said, pointing at Mercer, as if he'd proven something.

"Are you a campaign surrogate or something?"

Faunce let out a long, dramatic laugh. "I abhor politics. I'm simply trying to make people happy. I want to take care of the people of this great, forgotten part of our country. So, I bought them some clothes and asked Nan to hand them out to whoever wanted them."

Mercer finished his Take A Pop and tried not to grimace at the final dregs. "We should really grab the fireworks and be on our way. Our father's back at the house, waiting for us. Old guy, you know? Shouldn't be left alone too long."

"Of course, of course," Faunce said, though it was clear he was disappointed.

He walked them to the roundhouse's backyard, where he was keeping his mountain of fireworks. There had to have been ten thousand dollars' worth, all still in the packaging—bright, bold letters advertising the sheer power of Screaming Banshees, Gut Punchers, Improvised Explosive Demons, Death Spirals, and hundreds of other domestic weapons. "Feel free to take as much as you can grab. Or roll the car up. Whatever you'd like. It was purchased to be used by the people. There's nothing greater than seeing the sky lit up on our glorious nation's birthday."

"That's very kind of you," Evan said.

"These people have been overlooked for centuries. Just look at the way they're portrayed in the media. They're castigated as backward illiterates, incapable of making decisions for themselves."

Mercer tried his best to tune out Faunce and focus on the task at hand. He's just a crazy old man in the woods, he thought. Take as much as you can from him and tune out his words. Be more like Nan.

"There's a long history of discrimination against these people. You seem well-read, so I'm sure you know."

Evan shrugged.

"Are you familiar with James Fielder? Democratic governor from our great state. He toured these glorious woods in 1913 and returned to the capital. Do you know what he said?"

Mercer's arms were full, but he squatted down to grab a few more Bottle Rockets. "No, what did he say?"

"He suggested that these people be sterilized. He wanted them *e-rad-i-ca-ted*," Faunce said, drawing out each syllable of that final word. Evan wondered what had happened to the giddy eccentric from just a few minutes earlier. "That is *still* the opinion of the urban elite. They see these people as inconvenient—they see them as disposable."

There was a boom, followed by the shriek of a rocket taking flight. Faunce snapped out of his conspiratorial brooding and turned to take notice. He applauded, admiring the explosions above the house next door. "Sounds like this weekend's neighbors are making good use of the largesse! It doesn't matter who you are, what color your skin is, what god you worship—we're celebrating America. Aren't we?"

"Sure," Mercer said, walking in the direction of their car. "Who doesn't like to blow shit up?"

24.

Alejandra didn't know why it took her until 26 to realize something so obvious: these were bombs. She'd always loved fireworks on the Fourth but seeing them up close terrified her. She cupped her ears and walked in the opposite direction of Dave, who laughed as he shot another rocket towards the endless forest.

It was dumb, even irresponsible, to do this in the middle of the woods, especially in such a dry summer. Alejandra Googled the nearest fire department and wished she hadn't: it was almost an hour away. Still, she left the browser tab open and hoped she wouldn't need it, that she'd wake up hungover the next morning, confused about why she'd been so interested in the Southampton Fire Department.

She'd raised concerns an hour earlier when all of the bombs had been dumped on the dead lawn. "Maybe we wait until tomorrow," she'd said. "For the actual holiday." It was a diversion and an obvious one at that. A few of the others quietly agreed with her, but Dave wasn't having it. In his mind, it was simple. They were drunk in the middle of the afternoon and some creep in a dirty white suit had gifted them thousands of dollars of explosives. "The universe is practically begging us to have a good time," he'd said, and Alejandra had forced herself to laugh along with everyone else.

Before that weekend she hadn't known much about Dave other than that he worked in the Accounting Department and wore a Dri-fit polo every Friday, its breast emblazoned with the logo for his CrossFit gym. "It's practically my church," she remembered him saying.

She had never vacationed with co-workers before, though she didn't know that a long weekend at an Airbnb in the Pine Barrens was technically a vacation. The only person she'd ever known to consider it a getaway was Lake, who'd been so proud to buy his own "mountain house." When Alejandra had pointed out that the Pinelands were one of the flattest parts of the state, he'd rolled his eyes. "I apologize—my *cabin*."

Dave wanted a place where they could drink through the holiday with abandon. "We'll spend the weekend getting to know each other as people rather than as office mates. We will accomplish this through heavy drinking and general debauchery," he'd explained in the email. "It's our patriotic duty."

She hadn't planned on being there. She hadn't planned on anything beyond leaving Mercer the letter and then hiding out at her sister's until she figured out an actual plan. It was Maria who'd encouraged her to go. She'd even offered her the car, something Alejandra couldn't recall ever happening in the many years they'd lived near each other. "It'll be good for you," she'd said, though Alejandra knew that really meant it'd be good for Maria, whom she knew was already regretting offering her house as a landing pad.

That first night Maria demanded they finish a bottle of wine and "talk it out" while Tom set up the air mattress in the office.

She humored her sister but went to bed after only one glass, her stomach so tight that she couldn't even enjoy the expensive Malbec her sister had bought. Upstairs, she lay on the air mattress for what felt like hours, staring at the water damage on the ceiling. She wondered what Mercer was doing just a few blocks away in their house. She wanted to see him, to make sure that he was okay. Part of her thought he might be relieved, that maybe after the initial shock had worn off he'd realize that he didn't have to fight anymore—that an entirely new future was ahead of him.

Maybe he was excited. Maybe he was playing video games or jerking off or whatever else he did whenever she was gone. Maybe he was smiling.

25.

Mercer was determined to get back to their dad's cabin as soon as possible. The warmth of the gummy had faded, and he was looking forward to settling into a lawn chair, getting sufficiently hammered, and watching his father light up the July night.

But as they pulled away from Faunce's house, he had to slow down. It seemed impossible, but there it was in plain sight—Maria's busted Civic with the obnoxious, oversized PENN ALUMNA sticker on the rear window. Part of him wanted to keep driving, to spend the rest of the night telling himself it'd just been his imagination, but he couldn't help himself. He slammed on the brakes, sending Evan flying forward in the passenger seat, just short of banging his head on the dash.

His brother had been admiring the neighbors' fireworks display a few seconds earlier, but now he was massaging the side of his neck, as if that'd cure the whiplash. "Have you lost your mind?"

Mercer put the car in reverse and sped backward. When he was parallel with the Civic, he got out and walked up to it.

"The fuck are you doing?" Evan said. A firework exploded in the sky over the car and the pop echoed for what sounded like miles.

Mercer peered through the Civic's window for clues, but all he found were a few crumpled papers on the dash, some dirt on the floor, and a half-empty Diet Coke in the cup holder. He took out his phone and called Maria. She answered after one ring. "Are you trying to taunt me into filing that restraining order?" He could hear Tom in the background, passively asking her to lower her voice.

"Did you follow me to the Pines?"

"What?"

"I'm staring at your car, Maria. It's here, in the middle of nowhere New Jersey. You asked me to leave you alone, but now you're the one who's antagonizing me."

"Mercer, I think you should hang up," Evan said, leaving the car and walking towards his brother. There was another boom, followed by the sizzle of sparks falling back to earth.

"I'm with Tom, in the city," Maria said. "No one is following you."

The line went dead, and Mercer stared at his phone, unsure of what to do next. Then it hit him. He couldn't believe it, but he knew it had to be true. "She's here," Mercer said. He put his face against the glass. All he needed was a closer look to prove he was right.

Evan knew he needed to be delicate. He approached his brother with slow footsteps. "Who's here, Merce?"

Mercer recognized that voice—it was the high-pitched, soft touch his brother used when they were younger, the patronizing tone he'd deploy after he'd realized he'd taken a joke too far. It was what he'd used when he wanted to try and avoid the wrath of their parents.

Mercer wasn't interested in playing little brother. He wasn't the one who needed help. "It's Maria's car, I know it," he said. "She's not here, but Alejandra is."

Evan was closer now, close enough to grab his brother by the shoulders if he needed. "It could be anyone's car, bud."

"No. The sticker, the plates. All the same dents. It's Maria's. I don't know why Alejandra wound up here with her sister's car, but she did."

Father Brad had tried to prepare Evan for something like this. "Your brother is experiencing a trauma," he'd said when Evan first told him about the letter, about Mercer's kidnapping theory, about the way that his brother, for the first time he could remember, sounded like someone he didn't recognize. "He believes she's been kidnapped because he doesn't know how else to explain it."

"You're probably right, Merce. But there's a small chance you're not, and if some random Piney with Faunce's explosives finds us sniffing around his car…"

"*Her* car." Mercer was still glued to the window. "Alumna." There was another boom and Mercer stood back from the car to admire the rocket's golden stripes across the sky.

"What your brother needs is someone to help him now that he's not able to help himself," Father Brad had said. Evan remembered the way his brother had walked his dad through the endless paperwork of their mother's death. He remembered how he hadn't been strong enough to do it himself.

"I'm going into the house," Mercer said, still staring up at the sky, even though it was now blank.

Evan knew he needed to act. He knew he needed to help his little brother. “Mercer,” he said, grabbing him by the shoulder. Mercer turned and his brother recognized the vacant look on his face. He knows, Evan thought. He knows what I’m about to do. He knows I’m going to knock him out.

Part 3: The Air Tune

1.

You might've heard of the Jersey Devil. If you grew up in New Jersey, especially near the Pines, it might've even been taught to you. It's listed in some districts' curricula as "Relevant Local History" or "Regional Folk Storytelling," but the truth is most people just like stories about the Devil. It's even better when he's in the backyard.

There are different variations of the story, but most of them begin with Mary Leeds, a mother of 12 who was heartbroken when she learned she was pregnant with a 13th. The labor was so painful for that 13th child that she spent the whole miserable ordeal screaming that it was a devil. Once the thing had been pooped out, she realized she'd been right: on the ground between her legs was a horrible, winged beast. For a brief moment, she met its eyes and asked herself, could I love this thing? Before she could answer her own question, it let out a blood-curdling scream and flew off into the wild of the Pines.

That was back in 1735. For over a century it was little more than a folktale, something that explained randomly slaughtered farm animals or the strange sounds Pineys heard in the dead of night. But in 1909, newspapers in Trenton and Philly claimed there was undeniable proof the beast actually existed. Lonely grandmothers swore to reporters they'd heard its hooves ambling on their roofs. Children told stories of seeing the Devil soar through the sky over Pakim Pond. In response, hordes of men, probably bored and definitely drunk, formed militias, wandering the Pines in search of the thing. Aspiring Piney entrepreneurs affixed horns to their goats and charged only a few cents to see the real, live Jersey Devil.

These days, it's mostly a marketing strategy. No one owns the rights to the Jersey Devil, which means everyone does. The New Jersey Devils are a lackluster hockey team. Jersey Devil Auto is a reliable mechanic in Little Egg Harbor. The Jersey Devil Burger at the Jersey Devil Pub & Grill in Galloway is a bacon cheeseburger with mushrooms.

Some people still believe it's out there, lurking in the Pines. There's a man in Shamong who considers himself a Jersey Devil hunter. I emailed a few years ago and told him I wanted to join him on a hunt sometime. He gave me his home address and a time to meet but when I showed up at his house, a rickety colonial in the middle of the woods, no one was home. I called him several times and got no answer. The next morning, I emailed him again, telling him we could reschedule, but he never replied. I still don't know what happened. Sometimes I search for his name and then the word "obituary." I'm not saying he was killed by the Jersey Devil. I'm not, though I have thought that before.

There are so many different versions of the story that it's hard to keep track. Some claim the Devil is reptilian, scaly. Others say it's part kangaroo, part goat, or part horse. It all depends on which account you're reading.

There does seem to be one constant: all of the Devil's origin stories trace it back to Mary Leeds and her cursed pregnancy. Some go even further, claiming she was a witch, and her 13th child was Satan's. I think that's an unnecessary complication of a pretty good story. Do witches really want to sleep with Satan? Does Satan even have a penis?

You see what I mean? No one knows the answers to these questions. And, sure, it's all fiction, so maybe it doesn't matter. Maybe your interpretation of the Jersey Devil says a lot more about you than anything else.

But there's one aspect of the story that's not open to debate. Not for me at least. Mary Leeds was no witch. I don't believe she possessed any supernatural powers. No, I'm convinced Mary Leeds was just a worn-down mom trying to do her best. Any story that suggests otherwise isn't just a myth, it's a lie.

2.

It dawned on her a few months earlier in Maria's kitchen. They were washing dishes while their husbands sat in the living room, tasting bourbon Mercer had purchased that afternoon at Fine Wine & Good Spirits. It was rare or smoked or barrel-aged or maybe all three. All Alejandra remembered was it sounded overpriced.

"When did we become so domestic?" she asked her sister. She'd meant it as a joke, but as it left her mouth she knew it sounded like disappointment.

Her sister didn't blink. "What, because we're cleaning up while they jerk each other off?" Alejandra laughed, but her sister still sensed an uneasiness. "We trade nights. It's mine tonight. I mean, come on. I'm not a Stepford."

"No, I know. Bad example."

"All right. Give me a good one."

Alejandra was silent for a beat. "You just bought a dog."

"Okay..."

"Dog ownership is a test run for a baby."

"Here we go."

"And once you have the baby, you'll start talking about school districts. Which means you'll buy a house in the suburbs."

"Are these supposed to be bad things? You just described the aspirations of, like, 90% of the country."

"None of that depresses you?"

"Mom had next to nothing when she came here. She worked two jobs—"

"—during high school, yeah, I know—"

"—and I think it's a miracle if her grandkids can take advantage of what she wasn't able to."

They both fell silent, nervous about provoking the other any further. The guys were chuckling in the other room. "Must be a funny hand job," Alejandra said, but her sister didn't laugh.

"If you and Mercer want to continue to fuck off or whatever, that's fine, but don't make me feel bad about wanting normal things. You don't get to do that."

This always seemed to happen when Alejandra tried to have a frank conversation with her sister. Suggest there was more than one way to live, and it was interpreted as a personal affront. "I'm not trying to make you feel bad. I'm legitimately curious. I'm legitimately confused."

"What is there to be confused about? It's a pretty straightforward path. It's what most people choose. And it's not because they're conformists or sheep or whatever other condescending title you'd give them. It's because it's comfortable. And in a really uncomfortable world, chasing comfort isn't such a bad thing."

Alejandra nodded. She hoped it looked earnest because she didn't mean to upset her sister. "So, what comes after?"

"After what?"

"After your kid is in the nice school district and you've got the driveway and the yard."

"I don't know," Maria said, and then smiled. "We'll probably get another dog."

3.

Mercer couldn't remember the first time he heard the question. It had happened so many times that trying to recall the initial instance was like trying to recall when someone first asked for his name. He spent a few years awkwardly fumbling through responses, but after a while, he and Alejandra developed a list of stock answers.

QUESTIONER	RESPONSE
Mercer's parents' neighbors in National Park	"Hey, who knows?"
Extended family, especially Alejandra's	"We'll see!"
Co-workers, particularly Ms. Wanda at the library	"Didn't we just get married?"
Friends with children	"We really like sleeping in."
Friends without children	"Gross."

Eventually, Alejandra grew tired of keeping their plans secret. "We don't want kids," she started saying. It surprised everyone except for Mercer. They'd talked about it for years.

Children were great, but not for a lifetime. They were fun to see, but not to raise. Whenever their friends' toddlers erupted into uncontrollable tantrums, Alejandra and Mercer saw themselves out, waiting until their car doors were closed before laughing. "You *sure* you don't want kids?" Mercer would say.

It was a good plan. Separately their salaries weren't much,

but together they lived comfortably. They went out to dinner several times a week. They bought groceries from the overpriced store, the one that tried desperately to seem progressive, even though they both knew it was a rip-off. Who cared?

In a few years, they figured, they would be able to fuck off in Europe for a month. They were thinking about a vacation home in the next ten. Anything seemed possible, so long as it didn't include children.

Friends with kids took this stance as an insult, as if it were their children who had convinced Mercer and Alejandra to avoid procreating. No, Alejandra wanted to say, it's the thought of tearing myself in half.

"Have you considered adoption?" her dad asked them at the end of one Sunday dinner.

Unlike Mercer, Alejandra wanted her parents to know exactly where they stood. "We're just not interested in having kids," she said. "I'm sorry if that's upsetting for you." Mercer marveled at the way she was able to assert herself without ever raising her voice.

"Consider it. At the least consider it," her dad said. For the rest of dinner, he pushed around the food on his plate like a grounded teen. Before Mercer and Alejandra walked out the door, he made one more attempt. "The world needs more good parents," he said.

No, Alejandra wanted to say, the world doesn't need anything.

4.

Mercer hadn't planned on changing his mind. He also hadn't planned on his mom dying.

In the hours following the news, he longed for concrete objectives. He wanted to be of service, like he was doing something. He wanted to fix things, however small. So, he took the funeral proceedings from his dad, who wasn't so much upset as he was unresponsive. "You've made my life a lot easier," Lake told him, though the faraway look in his eyes remained.

Mercer contacted the parish and navigated the stupidly complex arrangements for a proper Catholic ceremony. He booked the National Park VFW for a luncheon, double-checking that they had enough Irish whiskey to keep his loudmouthed uncles happy. He bought his mother a casket and a plot and waved off the salesman's suggestion that he start a payment plan for the rest of the family.

His father couldn't stop thanking him. The aunts offered too many hugs and said how impressed they were with his assertiveness. Every night, Alejandra went out of her way to tell him how incredible he was, how he was making everyone's grieving just a little less painful.

But what Mercer had done was for the benefit of the living. He wanted to do something for his mother, even though she was gone, even though he didn't believe she'd wound up somewhere else, even though he'd ever really believed in somewhere else.

5.

Alejandra and Brigid were very different people. That was something Mercer said after each of their passive-aggressive standoffs.

"I'm aware," Alejandra would respond as she slammed the car door.

Mercer could sense when things had grown tense, but he could never spot the inciting action. They'd be at his parent's dinner table talking about the wedding and suddenly Mercer would feel the air grow thick. His dad would excuse himself, leaving Mercer to force polite conversation for the rest of the meal.

It wasn't until later that he was told the reasons. In the car, Alejandra would tell him that his mother had been making faces while she spoke. The next day on the phone, his mother would ask why Alejandra wasn't taking the family name. Alejandra would ask why his mother thought it was her place to criticize the bride's dress.

Mercer tried to maintain both allegiances, which of course only led to accusations of disloyalty on both sides. His father, meanwhile, wanted nothing to do with it. "Your mother's your mother," he'd say, and shrug.

"I just don't think you two are hearing each other," Mercer would say.

"I'm aware," Alejandra would say. "I'm aware that's what you think."

Alejandra wasn't sure women were supposed to get along with their mothers-in-law. Wasn't there some primal tension embedded in that relationship, of one woman taking the other's boy? She seemed to remember something like that from Intro to Anthropology. Or maybe it was Intro to Psychology. Freud, probably, though she also remembered her professor from Critical Theory saying that no one took Freud seriously anymore. Still: even if no dead white guy had said it, it was true.

She had girlfriends who went shopping and took spa days with their husband's moms. They gossiped, got wine drunk, and watched *The Bachelor*. It all sounded horrible.

Alejandra didn't need to be friends with Brigid, but she at least expected the outward performance of civility. When she first had dinner with Mercer's parents, she offered to help clear the table, but Brigid insisted she sit tight. "Please," she told her, "you're our guest." On their way out the door, she and Mercer thanked them for the meal. "It's our pleasure," Brigid said. "Maybe the next time you two can pitch in a little."

"It was a joke," Mercer said on the ride home. "It wasn't funny, but I swear it was a joke."

It took Alejandra a few years before she realized she'd never win over Brigid. In a way, it was comforting. There was nothing she could do. So long as she looked the way she did, Brigid would never see her as deserving of Mercer.

She figured Brigid didn't even know this about herself. She and Lake were lifelong Democrats, after all. "J.F.K. Catholics," Mercer had said when they'd first started dating, as if this was a term she'd heard before. Once upon a time they'd been "hippies," though Alejandra had always doubted the accuracy of that title. None of their stories of the past mentioned protests; they would've been in junior high during the Summer of Love. Her guess was what they really meant was they used to smoke a bunch of weed.

And Alejandra was sure Brigid believed the tension between the two of them had nothing to do with race. "Mercer's dating a Mexican girl," she imagined Brigid saying over the phone to some faceless relative, "which, of course, is *fine*."

She tried to broach the subject with Mercer, but he wasn't capable of hearing her. "You two got off-track somewhere and have struggled to pick up the pieces," he told her. She tried to be clearer, but no matter what words she used, he never seemed to receive them.

Alejandra wasn't so vain as to think she didn't have flaws. She could've been a little more gracious at Moore family functions, she guessed. She could've been more empathetic when the family talked about Evan's addiction—at the least, she knew she probably could've waited until she and Mercer were in the car to say she thought Lake and Brigid were enabling his behavior. She could have done that. Should have.

But she didn't know all that would've made a difference. Because it was the way Brigid's eyes squinted when she asked about the menu for their wedding. It was the way she mentioned differences in schooling or tradition or other convenient euphemisms. It was the way she slowed her speech the first time she met Alejandra's mother, as if she was doing this poor, pathetic immigrant a favor.

Beneath it all, Alejandra knew what Brigid was really trying to say. It was never spoken, but it was always loud: even just one drop of brown blood was far too much.

6.

People called Mercer's mom's death a "freak accident." It made it sound like she'd been run over by an 18-wheeler or mauled by wolves. It made it sound like no one could've predicted it, which was only partially true.

Aneurysms weren't accidents, they were events. And Brigid's aneurysm could've been predicted if she had been willing to say out loud that her own mother, who'd suffered an aneurysm a decade earlier, was more mirror than foil.

In that regard, Brigid's death made sense to Mercer. What didn't make sense was the way people who'd occupied such small spaces in her life seemed so irreparably damaged by her passing, like the way her estranged sister wailed during the funeral procession or how the voice of the choir's lead soprano quivered as he sang "One Bread, One Body."

Mercer couldn't summon the same intensity even though he felt the loss of his mother every minute of those months after she'd passed. She was the backdrop of every event, the subtext for all conversations. Out loud, though, it felt like vanity.

His earliest memory of a funeral was for his mom's father, a man he'd met exactly once in his life. "I need you to be strong for your mom today," Lake told him that morning. He was only six, but he knew what to do. When they arrived at the church he stood up straight, looked at a spot on the wall, and fixed his mouth into a perfect horizontal line.

After Mercer and Alejandra's wedding, Brigid mentioned

grandchildren in nearly every conversation. When they came across a unique name, she'd turn to Alejandra. "Maybe add it to the list, huh?" Lake talked about buying a shore house after retirement, but said he was waiting for something with enough bedrooms "for all the little ones." Mercer nodded through these conversations while Alejandra kicked his leg under the table.

It was too late to give his mother what she'd wanted. But his father was still alive. Maybe they'd get lucky and have a girl. Maybe they'd ignore the unique names that had become so popular with millennials. Maybe they'd go with something more traditional, something Gaelic, something like Brigid.

7.

After Brigid passed, Alejandra could feel herself stepping around conversations. She knew Mercer was grieving—of course, he was—albeit in that slow, private way the Moores did everything that required even the slightest bit of emotion.

The closest she'd been to grief had been walk-throughs at the wakes of distant relatives. There was an awkward, tense apology for the loss, a quick kneel at the casket to pray for a god who didn't exist, and then a swift exit. She hadn't had to live with grief, observing its subtle weight. She hadn't had to learn that it was barely visible but always present.

"Just be there for him," her sister had told her. And so, she was. She listened, sometimes for hours, on those rare instances when he wanted to talk about Brigid. Even then, there were never coherent stories, just disjointed fragments. He'd mention the way she'd sung "Tura Lura Lura" as a lullaby, then stop talking. He'd tell Alejandra how she'd write notes on his brown bag lunches through high school, then change the subject.

Maria had warned her that she needed to care for herself, too. "He's not the only one grieving," she'd said and widened her eyes, as if she was revealing a carefully guarded secret.

But Alejandra was fine. Yes, she was heartbroken by the way it affected Mercer and of course, she was horrified by the image of a woman's life ending on a cold, tile floor in a New Jersey kitchen. She wasn't haunted by Brigid's memory, though. She didn't regret the moments that would never happen.

It was tragic, but if you followed the string all the way to the end, weren't most things?

What she couldn't tell her sister—the person who held all of her most humiliating and destructive secrets—was that the most obvious feeling she'd noticed in the weeks following Brigid's funeral wasn't anything close to loss. It was relief.

When Mercer asked her to reconsider having a child, she assumed it was just the grief speaking—an irrational thought, a regret masked as desire. So, she deflected. "Let's talk in a few months," she told him. When he asked again a few months later, she pivoted. "Are we in a good place financially?"

She knew grief was unpredictable, but she hoped it would eventually fade into the background just like everything else. She was surprised to find that Mercer was unrelenting. He offered to babysit their friends' kids and opened a savings account labeled FAMILY FUND.

He explained it to her so many times—he hadn't realized he wanted to be a parent until he'd lost one. It was sweet, she knew. It was exactly what so many women her age wanted to hear.

It felt like a betrayal.

Alejandra tried to be as clear as possible in the letter. She didn't know that they were able to reconcile their differences. She was going away for a while. She didn't want him to contact her. She needed to figure some things out, for herself.

Alejandra put "rough draft" in the subject line of the email to her sister, though it didn't feel right. It made it feel like an assignment, like something she was submitting for feedback, even though she knew that this was final, that it was already happening.

After she sent it, her sister texted back quickly.

are you filing for divorce?

No. That's not what the letter says.

Did you read the whole email?

Alejandra went back to the email to re-read the attachment, worried that she hadn't been clear. That wasn't the issue; her sister was just being a moron.

Did you actually read it?

yes

and he's going to assume your asking for a divorce

She began to type a response, then stopped herself.

are you?!?!

8.

After the boys dropped him back at the cabin, Lake walked to the backyard to collect some kindling for the fire pit. He was pleasantly surprised to learn that he'd been right all along: the lumber guy had shown up late, but he had shown up. Every piece of wood needed for the deck was sitting on the lawn, laid out in four perfect stacks.

If he got started before the boys returned from their grocery run, they'd feel obligated to help him finish what he'd started. Evan would be hesitant, and Mercer would probably bitch, but they'd help him, even if it was out of pity.

He eyed the wood and planned his first move. He'd have to install the posts and then begin framing. It wasn't complicated, though it did require precision. He removed another gummy from the pouch in his pocket, chewing it as he began rooting through his toolbox.

He'd tried to teach the boys what he knew of the trades when they were younger, but the lessons never seemed to stick. They were amazed when he told them he'd practically built the first house he'd ever owned, but far less intrigued when he began to explain how he'd done it. National Park was working class through and through, but he knew his sons had grown up with a perspective much different than his own. They'd been sent to the high school outside of town, the one with the entrance exam. As a result, they'd always known they were headed for college, confident that their education would take care of them. They didn't need to learn how to replace pipes or apply drywall—they would always have enough money to pay someone else to do it.

It was what Lake had wanted. "Nothing is more important than education," he'd always told them when report cards arrived. He'd said the same when neighbors asked why Evan and Mercer didn't attend the public school.

Brigid had felt differently. The schools weren't cheap, and the family wasn't rich. They were Catholic, sure, but they could be Catholic with kids in the school district—with kids whose tuition didn't cost tens of thousands of dollars.

"We *have* the money," Lake had always said, as if they didn't read the same bank statements.

He was half right. They weren't poor, exactly, but there were months when their checking account remained unchanged. "Consistency," Lake would joke. "Isn't that a good thing?"

He hammered the posts into the holes and poured in the Quikrete. The bag said it should settle for 20 to 40 minutes, so he figured he'd give it 21. If the boys returned before he'd had a chance to start framing, then they'd tell him to wait until the morning. Then in the morning, they'd tell him to hire a contractor, some dumbass who'd charge $800 just to do it all wrong. He grabbed the last remaining beer from the fridge, dragged his Eagles chair from beside the fire pit over to his makeshift worksite, and waited.

He wondered what Brigid might make of the cabin. After

they'd had the boys, Lake and Brigid rarely imagined adventures for themselves. Sometimes they took the kids on day trips to Long Beach Island, but that was about all they had in terms of vacations. There were a few years when Brigid's parents invited the family to spend a week at their colonial in Cape May, though those invites ceased after Brigid and her mother stopped speaking. Thinking back on it, Lake couldn't even recall the reason for the falling out—they'd had so many blowouts over the years that all he could remember was one long contentious blur.

And that was what really terrified Lake. He could handle the isolation that came with being a widow. He didn't like being alone, but he had grown to appreciate the silence. He would sometimes spend an entire morning without uttering a single word. He found a strange comfort in it and wondered if that was what people meant when they talked about "serenity." But the idea that she'd start to disappear, that the finer details of his memories of her would begin to blend together into one lifeless, static photograph—that was what worried him.

The last time he'd swung by Arthur suggested keeping a journal, but Lake's attempts at cataloging who she'd been always fell painfully short of the real thing. He wanted to recapture the way she liked to hold his hand while he drove or how she'd develop a devilish smirk with her second glass of wine, but when he sat down in front of a blank page it all escaped him. The specific memories, the ones that mattered, only seemed to come when he was stoned, but when he was stoned the last thing he wanted to do was try to set words on a page.

The Quikrete only had five more minutes to go. Lake fastened the joists, so it'd be little more than assembly when the boys arrived. As he stood up, he felt the gummy in his legs, which wobbled under his body weight. He laughed at himself, shook off the brief disorientation, and went to his toolbox.

There was so much he wanted to ask her: if Evan was really as healthy as he seemed, if Mercer would be better off without Alejandra, if he'd been a fool to buy this backwoods cabin, if anything was ever going to feel normal again.

He hadn't used the nail gun in years; it felt heavy in his hands. Tools were like that. Working was like riding a bike. But wasn't the point of that analogy that riding a bike always felt the same? Unimportant, he thought. He held the joist down on the wood and tried to steady his aim.

At first, he didn't feel it. He stared at the nail, the one that'd just punctured the loose skin between his thumb and index finger, certain that he was imagining it. He tugged at it and felt his skin begin to tear. It wasn't until he saw the blood begin gushing out of his hand, that he realized he had a problem.

Lake's first instinct was to run, even though running didn't stop the frantic pulsing in his hand. It also didn't stop the blood, which was pouring from his body at a speed he didn't think was possible. As he sprinted away from the cabin, he could hear it splashing on the dirt behind him. It would be absorbed by the earth, he thought, just like everything else.

His nearest neighbor, Cato, was over a quarter mile away. Lake had only spoken with him once before, a few weeks after he'd bought the cabin. Cato had walked up the driveway unannounced with a soft cooler of Coors Light for the two of them. Lake didn't know that he'd ever met a black guy in a NASCAR shirt before, though he didn't say that. He didn't have to. "Bet you've never met a black guy in a NASCAR shirt before," Cato had said, and then took a sip from his beer.

They'd talked for a while and Cato said he'd keep an eye on the place when Lake was in National Park. "You ever need my help when you're here, you just swing by."

Lake turned towards his house, sprinting so hard that he thought he tasted iron in his throat. Cato was in the driveway, fiddling with a pickup on cinder blocks.

"Call an ambulance," Lake said between deep breaths.

Cato took his work gloves off and placed them on the roof of the truck. He approached Lake slowly, eyeing his hand. "They wouldn't be here for hours, frankly," he said. The blood was starting to pool on his driveway.

Cato removed his shirt and wrapped it around Lake's throbbing hand. "This is a start," he said, applying pressure with both of his hands. Lake eyed the shirt turning from white to pink and looked up at the shirtless Cato, whose chest hair was matted down with sweat. "You think you can take over?" Cato asked, gesturing to the shirt. Lake nodded, knowing there was no other answer.

Cato walked into the garage, disappearing into the unlit

cavern of toolboxes and random machinery. For a moment, Lake worried that Cato considered the problem solved. "I still think we should call an ambulance. Even if they're late. It might be good to check in." He wasn't sure if he was overreacting. A power tool shot a nail through your body, he reminded himself. He knew that technically, chemically, he was still stoned, but he was certain that the shock of the nail had snapped him back to sobriety. At least he was relatively certain.

Cato returned with a wooden spoon and a metal spatula and handed them both to Lake. He turned back to his truck and fumbled around the disorganized cab, detailing a story about how his last wife always told him if he'd cleaned up a little every day he wouldn't ever have trouble finding what he needed. Lake barely listened, focusing instead on the t-shirt wrapped around his hand, which was now a solid red. He let out a deep breath. The pulsing in his hand had also stopped. Maybe Cato had been right to stay calm. Maybe it had all been that simple.

Cato emerged from the cab with a flask and a long lighter. "Here we go!"

"I think it's stopped bleeding. It's definitely clotted," Lake said, though he didn't know that that was true.

"Figured it would. That's the first step." He placed the lighter under his arm and unscrewed the flask. "This is the next."

He removed the t-shirt from Lake's hand and poured the flask's liquid over the wound. Vodka, but maybe gin. Lake couldn't be sure from the smell. All he knew was that it was cheap.

Cato took back the spatula and held it above the lighter's flame. "Let's give it a minute," he said.

"I really think I'm all right," Lake said.

"Best way to make sure this doesn't start bleeding again is to cauterize it. I'm about to do that for free. Doctor in Hammonton is going to co-pay you out the ass."

It was a good word, "Cauterize." Lake had heard it before, several times actually, though he wasn't sure of the exact definition. He knew wounds were cauterized, but that was about it. It was a miracle this man had been there to save him, that he'd known exactly what to do without a modicum of panic. Even then, as he told Lake to put the wooden spoon in his mouth, he was remarkably calm.

Lake tasted the wood on his tongue and started to laugh. He didn't know why; Cato hadn't made a joke. No, all Cato said was "I'd turn away," and "It's always easier when you're not looking," and "Don't forget to bite down."

9.

Lake was back at work on the deck by the time Evan pulled into the driveway with an incapacitated Mercer slumped against the passenger side window. When the engine turned off, Mercer woke up in a panic. It was the music from his dad's boombox that told him he was back at the cabin. *Before you accuse me, take a look at yourself.*

Evan turned to his brother from the driver's seat. "I want you to know I'm sorry. We just had to get out of there."

Mercer didn't respond. He studied himself in the side mirror, delicately touching the purple-black oval around his eye.

"She might think you tracked her down, Merce. That you're *stalking* her. If you're hoping to win her back—"

"—stop talking." Mercer leaned closer so that OBJECTS IN MIRROR ARE CLOSER THAN THEY APPEAR floated over his bruise.

Lake started walking towards the car. "You bring me some beer? Need it more than ever," he said, raising his voice over Clapton's.

Evan left Mercer in the car and grabbed an armful of fireworks from the trunk. "Not quite. We got a bit sidetracked."

Lake laughed at the hundreds of explosives in his son's car. "Dear God. This is an arsenal."

"All Mercer. He made it happen. And for free." He hoped his brother heard that, even if he was trying to ignore him.

"The Moores! Making deals!"

Mercer opened the passenger door and stood to face his brother. "Can I have my keys back?"

"What the hell happened to your eye?" Lake squinted, studying every popped vessel.

"Your co-worker over here knocked me out."

Lake turned to Evan with a look that was equal parts admiration and confusion. "Quite the shot."

Evan grabbed a few more Cherry Bombs and a pack of Annihilators. "Are we celebrating the holiday or not?"

"Actually, while we've still got some daylight, I thought we could make some headway on the deck."

"Evan. My keys."

"I just know the two of you are leaving in the morning, and I can't do it myself. Especially now." Lake held up his hand to show Cato's cauterization. The rectangle of blistered black and orange skin took up his entire palm.

Evan gagged. He was certain he could smell the decay.

"Long story. But I'm good with my other hand, and we've still got a solid two hours until it's really dark," Lake said. "And who wants to do fireworks before then anyways?"

Mercer hadn't moved from his plot beside the car, not even at the site of his dad's rotting hand. "I want my keys, Evan."

"Dad, we've got to get you to a hospital." Evan took out his phone but realized he had no service. "There's got to be one nearby. Is there a neighbor we can talk to?"

"Nearest hospital is a waste of time. It's really nothing.

Cato says it always looks bad on the first day. That's how you know it's working. Actually, he told me a few beers would do the job just fine. So, maybe you could run back out the store…"

"Cato?"

"Evan!" Mercer screamed. The sound echoed through the backyard and into the Pines.

"Jesus Christ, Mercer, would you calm down? A nail went through my hand and I'm smiling. Maybe follow my example for once?"

"Fuck you, Dad."

"Excuse me?" Lake rubbed his dead hand like he was preparing to use it. "I don't know what you did to earn that black eye, but you're fixing to earn a second."

"You heard me." Mercer was speaking with a force his brother had never seen. It sounded like he was demanding something, even though he wasn't asking for anything. "Since Mom's been gone, I've done everything I could to help you. Because I knew Mom being gone killed you. I knew that. But you can't even be bothered to do the same for me."

"Let's all take a deep breath," Evan said.

It was a predictable pattern, one that'd existed for as long as Mercer could remember. His brother would create a problem, Mercer would respond, and then Evan would present himself as the rational mediator, the one who was just trying to make sure everyone get along. Once, when they were still in middle school, Mercer had tried explaining to his mother, how Evan didn't respect him, how he ignored everything Mercer said, how he seemed intent on watching him suffer. Brigid had nodded along. "You can't control other people," she'd said, holding both of his hands. "The only thing you can do is listen and then make yourself heard."

"Give me my keys, Evan," Mercer said again.

"I know what you're doing bringing your mother into this. I know exactly what you're doing."

Evan didn't know what else to say. "Let's all just take a deep breath."

Mercer closed his eyes and, sure enough, Evan saw him take a long, deep breath. It worked, Evan thought. I don't know why it worked, but it worked.

That was right before Mercer's eyes shot open, right before he stretched his arms out and pushed his older brother to the ground. Lake tried to grab both of them, to break up what he assumed was a knock-down drag-out fight like the kind they used to have in the backyard in National Park. But Mercer wasn't interested in rehashing the past. As soon as he saw an opening, he grabbed the keys from Evan's loosened grip and jumped in the car.

By the time Lake helped Evan back on his feet, Mercer was speeding down the dirt road, away from the cabin, back to Alejandra.

10.

Alejandra heard the knocking when she was inside, grabbing another drink. When she peeked out the side window, she didn't want to believe what she saw. She couldn't.

At first, she thought she'd be able to wait it out, but several minutes passed without Mercer breaking his four-four rhythm. She thought about asking Dave and the others to handle it, but she worried they might drunkenly misinterpret Mercer as a threat. If she sat with him on the porch, she thought, maybe she could calm him down. Maybe she could send him off on a positive note, without having to explain to her co-workers that the guy with the uneasy eyes banging on the front door was technically her husband.

A few days earlier she'd told her sister she thought she owed Mercer more than the letter, but her sister was adamant. "One surrender leads to another," she'd said. "You both want different things. Nothing's going to change that."

He smiled when she opened the door. That's when Alejandra knew it was a bad idea.

"How did you find me here?" she asked.

"I just wanted to see you. I just wanted to apologize for everything," Mercer said. "I know it's probably too late, but I wanted to let you know that I just quit the library."

"Just now?"

"On the way over. No one was in the office, but I left a voicemail letting them know I'm done."

"Why?"

Mercer didn't understand. "You spent months telling me to quit."

"I encouraged you to find something else if it'd make you happier."

"Exactly. So, after the library, I called Dane. Transformational Talks." Alejandra was still confused. "The Banana Boy. We're meeting up next week to talk about crafting a presentation on surviving my brother's addiction." When he heard himself say that out loud, Mercer tried to sound upbeat. He knew he was not convincing.

"Is that all you took away from my letter? That I wanted you to get a new job?"

Mercer knew what this meant. "Not the only thing," he lied. He tried to recall her exact words, but all he could remember was Alejandra's distinct handwriting on the tri-folded pages.

"Why did you report me as missing?"

In the absence of an answer, he blinked. He hoped the question was rhetorical, but Alejandra's silence told him it wasn't. "I just couldn't imagine you writing that letter," he said.

Her sister wanted her to be angry with Mercer—for never taking her side, for never considering her feelings, for terrifying her family with calls from the police, for showing up drunk and talking shit. And she was angry, she supposed, though it was a tiny feeling compared to what she felt when she looked at his flushed face, desperate to hang on to everything from the past, even if it was broken and could never be fixed.

That bigger feeling, the one that was filling up the majority of her chest, was something much worse than anger. It was pity.

11.

Evan didn't know where to begin. On the phone, Alejandra told him Mercer had stormed off and that she had no idea where he was headed. "He didn't seem well," she said. It was not Alejandra's fault, Evan reminded himself. He knew it wasn't, even though he wished it was.

Lake wanted to call the cops, but Evan talked him down. Mercer had already had one run-in with the law. He imagined a second encounter wouldn't end with another complimentary ride home. Evan called his brother's phone, again and again, hanging up every time he heard the first words of Mercer's voicemail message. *Hi, you've—. Hi, you've—. Hi, you've—. Hi, you've—.*

He told his father to get in the car with the confidence of someone who had a plan. He would figure it out once they began driving. In the meantime, that's all he could do—drive around the sand roads as the sun disappeared and pray for divine intervention.

It was after 38 minutes into the non-plan when his father finally spoke up. "I know I don't talk about her much," he said.

"I don't think Mercer meant that, Dad. He's just worked up. He's all over the place."

Lake was still staring out the window. "It just never feels like the right time, does it?"

"No," Evan said. He tried to find something else to say, something more than one syllable, but everything else felt trite.

It never felt like the right time to talk about his mother because there would never be enough time to explain all of who she'd been.

When he'd been "asked to leave" college she'd sighed, folded up the letter, handed it back to him, and told him she loved him. It was the same when he'd received his first DUI. "Tell me how I can help you," was all she'd said. He knew she'd probably screamed in the empty house after hanging up or took it out on some poor cashier at the supermarket the next day, but in that moment she'd wanted Evan to know that all she had for him was endless, undying love.

He remembered so few specifics from her funeral, though there were still enough in his memory to know he should be embarrassed. Mercer had filled him in on what had been blacked out, providing context for the scenes that took place between the snapshots. This had not been done to make Evan feel better, he knew.

There was a part of him that wished she'd abandoned him. He'd heard it so many times in meetings—parents using tough love, kicking out their drunk kids, teaching them hard lessons. It would've given him something to hold on to, something that he could use to remind himself that she wasn't perfect either. But that was a small part of him, and it was one that he hoped was getting smaller.

12.

Sammy Giberson was a good fiddler and a half-decent dancer. These were not his most obvious personality traits. Mostly, he was a drunk and a shit-talker. These things usually go hand-in-hand.

One night at a tavern in the Pines, he bragged that he could beat anyone at fiddling and dancing—even the Devil. He didn't know why he got like that. When he wasn't drinking, he was a relatively quiet guy. But talking loud in the tavern just made things a bit more interesting, even if it put some people off. He was turning all this over in his mind on his stumble home when he came to a swamp bridge. And who was waiting there?

Come on. It was the Devil. You knew that.

"Heard you've been talking shit," the Devil said.

"Yeah, well," Sammy replied.

The Devil challenged him to some fiddling. Sammy was good, but not great. The Devil's song, on the other hand, sounded better than anything Sammy had ever heard. Sammy tried dancing, but he'd had one too many at the tavern and tripped over his own feet. The Devil laughed and offered a flawless jig in return. His hooves clopped on the wooden bridge, ringing out through the night like a gavel.

"As payment for your boasting, you're coming back to Hell with me," the Devil told him. "Unless you can play a song I've never heard before."

Sammy was surprised—he didn't think the Devil was the

type to offer second chances. He started to think that maybe the stories had been wrong. You know, the ones about vengeance and hatred and fire and brimstone and all that. He'd never even met the Devil before that night, yet he'd assumed so much about him.

Then he remembered: eternal damnation unless you find a song. Right. Need to find a song.

A strong wind blew through the Pines, shaking the trunk of every tree Sammy could see. Over his head, there was the faint hint of a melody. He looked at the Devil's red face to see if he heard it, too, but the beast didn't seem to notice anything strange. "Do you have a song or not?" was all he said.

Sammy closed his eyes and tried to focus on the sounds passing over his head. When he was sober he was silent and when he was drunk he was obnoxious. But now he tried listening, which was unlike either of those more passive ways of being. It required real effort and care. It was exhausting.

But it worked. He picked up his fiddle and played along with the air, mimicking its immaculate tune as best as he could. When it was over, he opened his eyes to find the Devil with tears running down his red cheeks. Sammy's song was the most beautiful thing he'd ever heard.

13.

There was just enough daylight for Mercer to find the trailhead. He hadn't been interested in it earlier, when he'd walked on the same sand with his brother and father, but now he felt drawn in by the woods. The tea-colored water of the bogs seemed otherworldly. The slender white oak seemed like an installation. It was a miracle, he realized. Despite all of the magic in front of him, he was still in New Jersey.

She found him a few miles into the woods, stopping him in the middle of the trail with a smile. Her crewcut, an uneven mess that looked like it'd been done with her own shaky hands, convinced him that she was a young man, still under the drinking age, still too young to care about such a shitty haircut. "Things are pretty muddy a half mile up," she said. "Going to be dark by the time you get there." It was when she spoke that he realized she was a woman. Her voice told him that he shouldn't be concerned, even though he was miles away from civilization.

Mercer nodded like he was going to heed her advice, though he had no idea whether or not he'd give up in the next half mile. He had no idea about anything. "Appreciate it," he said.

"Probably from all that rain last night." She carried a camo pack and wore fatigues that looked like they were inherited from someone three times her size. The canvas was crusted with mud stains, as if she'd been crawling her way down the trail.

"Practically washed me out. I spent at least two hours this morning just drying out all my gear."

Mercer remembered Nan's brick and the police escort back to the cabin, but he didn't remember a storm. "It rained?"

"Were you on the trail last night?"

"No."

"Okay," she said, as if the answer was obvious. "So maybe that's why you don't remember the rain?" She adjusted the straps of her rucksack and Mercer heard the subtle clang of pots and pans.

"You hiking the whole thing?

"Whole thing, then back," she said. "Then the whole thing again, then back again. Then likely the whole thing again, then back again."

"By yourself?"

She nodded with pride. "My family's all military. Grandpa was a Green Beret. Father was 17th Infantry. Mother was Air Force. Brother was Coast Guard. Sister was Merchant Marine. It's in my blood. It's not easy, but it feels natural. I think some things are just inherited. Some things are beyond us. I think you know what I mean."

He didn't. "Totally," he said. He licked his plastic teeth and hoped she wasn't capable of harm.

"It wasn't all easy. My first few days were rough, honestly. But then I started thinking outside of myself. I started turning my mind off. And what I noticed was that once I was able to turn that off, I was suddenly in tune with something much,

much larger. Do you follow me, Mercer?"

He wasn't sure he'd heard her correctly. "Did you say my name?"

"I've learned everything I need by taking in my surroundings. There's a man a few miles down the trail who built a house out of fallen pines. You won't be able to see it from the trail, but you'll know you're close when you hear the barking of his dog. And this," she said, holding up a slender branch, "this points towards fresh water. As long as I trust its guidance, it will sway in the direction of a spring. Do you believe that?"

Mercer wasn't sure she was speaking to him. He wasn't sure she was there. So much of the time leading up to that moment had felt like a dream that he was no longer sure if he was sleeping or waking.

"As you continue walking," she said, as Mercer closed his eyes, "I want you to know that if you need help, you just need to listen. That's how you find help. That's all you need to do—wherever you are. You need to listen."

By the time Mercer opened his eyes, night had arrived. The woman was gone. He wasn't sure that she'd been there in the first place. He wasn't sure of anything, really, other than that he'd driven to the woods to go get lost in the darkness.

In the parking lot, Mercer's phone buzzed two times, even though he wasn't there to hear it.

thats all you need to do

14.

She had forgotten how refreshing actual silence could be. Even the backyard, where she'd dug out a garden as an excuse to have some time for herself, was never truly quiet. There was the chirping of a few birds on the low-hanging electrical wires and the long drone of commercial planes on their way to the airport. And there was Alan, just on the other side of the wooden fence, blaring classic rock radio and doing whatever it was that required him to spend long days in his yard, despite the weather or the sanity of his neighbors.

But the car was different: it felt hermetic, sterile, like she'd been sealed off by a team of specialists, intent on preserving what remained of her.

It all happened so quickly. The boys were uncontrollable like always, something her mother had pointed out with every visit. "She was trying to relate," Lake had said, as if after five years he understood her mother better than she did. "She was trying to connect. Mom-to-mom."

Lake had the ability to see things as he wanted them to be rather than how they were. There were times when Brigid envied that. It was one of the things that'd drawn her to him so many years earlier. It was how he'd convinced her that the most exciting thing they could do was start a family. Lately, though, his undying optimism felt like a betrayal. All she wanted was for him to trust that she wasn't just being negative, she was drowning.

She knew that if she tried to explain what had happened with the boys, he wouldn't hear it. Evan hadn't intended to hurt Mercer, he'd say. He hadn't been malicious when he aimed for the cast on his younger brother's arm, the one that'd just been molded the day before. He hadn't fully understood the gravity of his actions, hadn't smiled as he grabbed Mercer's arm with two hands and shook his tender bones.

He was just a kid. They were just being boys. "If you could've seen what my brothers did to me," Lake would say.

A cadre of power-walking moms passed Brigid's car, which was still parked in the driveway. They pumped their arms in unison and she could hear the swish-swish of their windbreakers, the soundtrack to their neighborhood gossip. One of the women waved at Brigid, who forced a smile back.

This wasn't the first time it'd felt like this. A few years earlier she'd had enough of the toys strewn across every inch of the carpets, the cracker crumbs in every imaginable crevice, the fact that dusting every Saturday never actually prevented dust from reappearing on every surface by Sunday morning. She'd told the men in her life that she was tired and underappreciated. She didn't know what she needed, but she knew what she could no longer take.

"I'm going on strike," she'd said one night at dinner. By that point, Lake knew better than to tell her to "calm down" or "take a deep breath," but not enough to do anything other than say he'd take the kids camping for the weekend, that she should go to a spa or see her sister or something.

She knew the power-walking moms felt this way, too, even if they'd never admit it. It was one of the last taboos, she thought. We can talk about abortion and anal but if we say we're worried we've grown to hate our children we have to couch it in a laugh. We have to clarify that it was just one of the rare "bad days." Even there, alone in the car, she couldn't imagine saying the words out loud.

She loved them. Of course, she did. But "love" was such an easy word—a cop-out disguised as a catch-all. It was a complicated signifier that no one ever wanted to untangle. It meant that Lake understood her more than anyone she'd ever met and yet could still misunderstand her so profoundly. It meant she could adore Mercer's gentleness and yet be disappointed in the way he let the world push him around. It meant she could call Evan her heart and still relish the sound of her palm striking his face. It meant she could hold him down by his shoulders and tell him he didn't have the right to treat his brother that way—he didn't have the right to treat anyone that way—and still be a good mom.

Because she was. She was a good mom.

She didn't know that she'd actually planned on driving away. She'd grabbed the keys and run to the car, but then she'd thrown them in the cup holder and sat in the driver's seat, incapable of taking the next step. She would later tell herself the whole thing had been an unconscious reaction—she would use the terms "sleepwalking," "autopilot," other words that made the distance between herself and her actions as wide as possible.

She would apologize. She would tell Evan she'd made a mistake—that we never use violence to solve our problems, that even adults get angry sometimes. She would call Lake at work and relay the story, praying that such visceral aggression might finally make sense for him. She would hope that Mercer would not mention any of it to his kindergarten teacher, a well-intentioned but naive 24-year-old who would never understand that this was not child abuse.

She would go back inside, and she would stay there. She would take deep breaths and see if she could do a few mornings with the power-walking moms. She would see the other side, even if there wasn't one.

15.

Mercer expected stillness, but the Pines were alive: frogs yelled across the creeks, foxes stomped on fallen leaves, deer jogged down sand paths and up Apple Pie Hill, trying to see if they could catch a glimpse of Atlantic City's neon lights.

He was awed by the volume, the way the Pines spoke even if no one was there to listen. He wanted to be a part of it but worried he might make it all run scared, shut it down, shut it up. So, no, he would just remain a member of the audience. He would drag his hands across the moss. He would lay down on the sugar sand, even though it was damp. He would stare up at the navy sky and listen to the Pines.

Mercer knew he would move on someday. It would be painful, of course, and painful in a way that he'd never known before. His brother would tell him that "it would just take time." It was a cliché, and it'd anger Mercer in the moment, but it was also true. It had to be.

Because everything took time. He would survive the next year or two or three, and then he would move on, start seeing people, get to a point where he could call Alejandra a friend and mean it. It would all sound easier when Evan said it.

It would take time, as in it would take time away from him. The best he could hope for was that this period of his life would pass by in a blur. He would pray for the mercy of forgettable days. He would accept that it was all he could do.

He would eventually be found—through the sounds of the

night he'd hear the faint hum of his father and brother calling his full name, over and over and over again. He would stand up, wipe the sand from his arms and call back until they found him with their flashlights. He'd embrace them, clasping tight with his balled fists, and assure them that he was all right or at least as all right as he'd been that weekend.

He imagined Evan smiling. He pictured his Dad holding back tears. He'd tell them that he wanted to be better, that he had a list of things he'd accomplish that next morning, that he was already imagining the index card, that he'd realized the only thing stopping him was himself.

And he'd really mean it. Really.

And even if there was a part of him that didn't, he'd tell that part to quiet down. He'd tell it to try and listen for once.

Acknowledgments

Mom and Dad, thank you for everything. You both taught me to love books and showed me the power of writing. Brian, Brendan, Mike, and Sheila, thanks for putting up with me. Love to the extended Kearney, Herrick, Lewis, and Welch clans.

I'm fortunate to be surrounded by wildly inspiring and creative people. Many of those folks read early versions of this book, offering feedback and encouragement: Cristian Adams, Sean Close, Samantha Combs, Nat Harting, Tyler and Emily Jeffries, Alex Moxam, Holly and Julien Rossow-Greenberg, Kelsey Ruane, Sean and Caroline Spencer, and Nikki Volpicelli. Special thanks to Kevin Comly and Jessie Gemmer for lending their handwriting and to Mike Thackray for lending his eyes!

Jordan M. Mrazik not only designed the cover, but also acted as an invaluable sounding board who made me think differently about the possibilities of this story.

Thank you to Josh Dale at Thirty West for believing in this book and to Kat Giordano for being such a gracious editor.

And thank you to Sloane, who is and has always been my best friend and most enthusiastic champion. I love you.

Thanks for reading. It was good spending time with you.

About the Author

Kevin M. Kearney grew up in New Jersey. His writing has appeared in *Pithead Chapel*, *Hobart*, *X-R-A-Y*, and elsewhere. *How to Keep Time* is his first novel.

More at kevinmkearney.com

About the Publisher

Thirty West Publishing House

Handmade Chapbooks (and more) since 2015

www.thirtywestph.com / thirtywestph@gmail.com

You should follow us and consider being a patron!

Review our books on Amazon & Goodreads

@thirtywestph

CPSIA information can be obtained
at www.ICGtesting.com
Printed in the USA
BVHW071810101022
648878BV00004B/11

9 798986 110516